## *Anna's heart skipped a beat.*

Even through her wedding veil, his gaze pinned her in places like an electric-blue laser.

He reached into his inside jacket pocket and pulled out a cell phone. He stopped to talk, his riveting eyes never leaving her.

Anna leaned in close to her friend, fighting off panic. "He's the perfect male," she whispered, her voice shaky.

Before she could say another word, her "groom" stepped closer, cell phone in hand. His well-over-six-foot frame towered her.

"Well, well," he drawled, giving Anna an intense once-over. "You must be my bride."

Anna took his extended hand. "Anna…Si…mpson," she managed, using her fake last name.

"Ryan Cavanaugh." He shook her hand and flashed a blinding smile. Deep dimples formed on both sides of his mouth. He leaned in closer to her. "Lucky me."

Dear Reader,

If you're like me, you can't get enough heartwarming love stories and real-life fairy tales that end happily ever after. You'll find what you need and so much more with Silhouette Romance each month.

This month you're in for an extra treat. Bestselling author Susan Meier kicks off MARRYING THE BOSS'S DAUGHTER—the brand-new six-book series written exclusively for Silhouette Romance. In this launch title, *Love, Your Secret Admirer* (#1684), our favorite matchmaking heiress helps a naive secretary snare her boss's attention with an eye-catching makeover.

A sexy rancher discovers love and the son he never knew, when he matches wits with a beautiful teacher, in *What a Woman Should Know* (#1685) by Cara Colter. And a not-so plain Jane captures a royal heart, in *To Kiss a Sheik* (#1686) by Teresa Southwick, the second of three titles in her sultry DESERT BRIDES miniseries.

Debrah Morris brings you a love story of two lifetimes, in *When Lightning Strikes Twice* (#1687), the newest paranormal love story in the SOULMATES series. And sparks sizzle between an innocent curator—with a big secret—and the town's new lawman, in *Ransom* (#1688) by Diane Pershing. Will a seamstress's new beau still love her when he learns she is an undercover heiress? Find out in *The Bridal Chronicles* (#1689) by Lissa Manley.

Be my guest and feed your need for tender and lighthearted romance with all six of this month's great new love stories from Silhouette Romance.

Enjoy!

Mavis C. Allen
Associate Senior Editor, Silhouette Romance

Please address questions and book requests to:
Silhouette Reader Service
U.S.: 3010 Walden Ave., P.O. Box 1325, Buffalo, NY 14269
Canadian: P.O. Box 609, Fort Erie, Ont. L2A 5X3

# The Bridal Chronicles

## LISSA MANLEY

SILHOUETTE *Romance*®

Published by Silhouette Books

America's Publisher of Contemporary Romance

This book is dedicated to my wonderful husband, Kevin,
who supported me through nine years
of the ups and downs of an aspiring author.
Thanks for all the Tuesday nights.
I love you.

 SILHOUETTE BOOKS

ISBN 0-373-19689-X

THE BRIDAL CHRONICLES

Copyright © 2003 by Melissa A. Manley

**Books by Lissa Manley**

Silhouette Romance

*The Bachelor Chronicles* #1665
*The Bridal Chronicles* #1689

---

## LISSA MANLEY

has been an avid reader of romance since her teens and firmly believes that writing romances with happy endings is her dream job. She lives in the beautiful Pacific Northwest with her college-sweetheart husband of nineteen years, Kevin, two children, Laura and Sean, and two feisty toy poodles named Lexi and Angel, who run the household and get away with it. She has a degree in business from the University of Oregon, having discovered the joys of writing well after her college years. In her spare time, she enjoys reading, crafting, attending her children's sporting events and relaxing at the family vacation home on the Oregon coast.

Lissa loves to hear from her readers. She can be reached at P.O. Box 91336, Portland, OR 97291-0336, or at http://lissamanley.com.

## A Pretend Bride's To-Do List:

- ❤ Spend as little time as possible with the pretend groom so as not to fall under his spell. We know what happens to you around good-looking men.

- ❤ Pay no attention to his stunning smile and gorgeous eyes and seemingly generous personality.

- ❤ Get the pretend ceremony over with.

- ❤ Forego pre-pretend-wedding jitters. This is a fake wedding!

- ❤ Try not to worry about the cameras…. The tabloids won't even think to come here. Will they?

# Chapter One

Anna Sinclair looked across the Rose Garden Park through her veil and raised a shaky hand to her throat. She watched the tall, incredibly handsome hunk stride confidently toward her.

Smiling, he paused to talk to the pretty, female photographer's assistant, and his dark blond hair glinted like gold in the midmorning June sun. Dark green, leafy foliage, framed by the cloudless blue summer sky, provided the perfect backdrop for his stunning male beauty. His black tuxedo, hugging his wide-shouldered, athletic body like a glove, made him look like every bride's dream come true.

But not Anna's. Designing wedding dresses was as close as she would ever get to that romantic nonsense.

Wondering if she was an utter fool for getting anywhere near a camera, or a gorgeous man like that, she looked to Colleen Stewart, the tall, blond reporter assigned to "The Bridal Chronicles," a newspaper special feature. "Please tell me that male model is not my groom.'' Anna gestured to the god across the lawn, his head bent in thoughtful discussion, one hand casually shoved into the pocket of his tuxedo pants.

Colleen fluffed the train on Anna's dress and looked in the direction she had gestured. Colleen whistled under her breath and her blue eyes gleamed. ''He's not a male model, Anna, even though he looks like one. His name is Ryan Cavanaugh and he's the wealthy owner of a local chain of coffee houses, Java Joint. The Bachelor Chronicles was so successful featuring Jared Warfield, who owns a competing chain of coffee stores, that we decided to feature another coffee guy.'' She put a hand on Anna's arm. ''Don't tell me you have a problem posing with good-looking men.''

Anna spun around, inadvertently ruining the billowing train Colleen had taken so long to arrange. ''Yes, I do.'' Good-looking men always made her do foolish things. ''I only agreed to pose because the woman originally scheduled to wear my gown didn't show up.''

''So, what's the problem?'' Colleen asked. ''You want your gown in the spread, right?''

''Of course I do. I'm hoping that my gown being in 'The Bridal Chronicles' will help me land that account I've come to Portland to acquire.'' Landing the Perfect Bridal account was her last chance to fulfill the terms of her father's deal.

She took a deep breath, telling herself to calm down. ''But when I agreed to pose at the last minute, I didn't anticipate that my groom would be so…so gorgeous. What if we win Best Wedding Couple?''

''Then you pose for more pictures and your gown gets more publicity.''

*More pictures.* Concealing her real identity with a veil for *one* picture was going to be risky enough, even though she'd dyed her dark brown hair auburn and by some miracle Colleen hadn't recognized her. "More pictures would be very bad," Anna said under her breath. "Very, very bad."

"Actually, with a hunk like Ryan around, I imagine it'll be very, very good."

"Yes, indeed." Anna fluffed her dress, needing air circulation. "It'll be too good, and we'll be a shoo-in for Best Wedding Couple." She fanned herself with her hand, convinced the warm June sun was getting to her. Would anyone notice a woman in a pristine white wedding gown, her face fully covered by a fluffy veil, sneaking off before any pictures could be taken?

She should have never agreed to this. She certainly didn't want to end up where well-known heiresses often did—on the front page of a tacky tabloid, the subject of an unflattering picture for all the world to see. "I assumed I'd be posing for one picture. Nothing more."

"Just relax," Colleen soothed. "You have no way of knowing who's going to be voted Best Wedding Couple."

"No way of knowing? Look at him." Anna followed her own instructions and looked back to this Ryan guy. He'd left the fluttery-eyed assistant, who looked like she was about to melt into a pool of water on the lush, rolling lawn of the Rose Garden, and he was again striding confidently toward Anna and Colleen. With smooth male grace, he casually unbuttoned his tux jacket, staring at Anna. Even through her veil, his gaze pinned her in place like an electric-blue laser.

Her heart missed a beat.

He reached into his inside jacket pocket and pulled out a cell phone. He stopped to talk, his riveting eyes never leaving her.

She ripped her gaze from him and leaned in close to Colleen, fighting off panic. "He's the perfect male," she whispered, her voice shaky. "Every woman in the city will be wiping away drool as they cast their vote for him." She shook her head. "I'm not sure this is a good idea." Yes, she wanted her gown in the photo spread. But not if it would reveal her real identity. She was simply humble working girl Anna Simpson, designer of the Anastasia line of wedding dresses for the time being. She didn't want anyone to know she was really Anna Sinclair, the daughter of one of the richest bankers in the country. How would she know if she were a true success if the Sinclair name followed her around?

Colleen pressed a hand to Anna's arm. "Please don't leave me in the lurch. I'll never find another model on such short notice."

A shaft of familiar guilt poked Anna. Her father always made her feel like she was letting him down, too. Before she could reply, her "groom" stepped closer, cell phone in hand. His well over six-foot frame towered above both her and Colleen.

"Well, well," he drawled, giving Anna an intense once-over. "You must be my bride." He extended his hand. "Ryan Cavanaugh."

She took his hand. "Anna...Si...mpson," she managed to say, using the fake last name she'd come up with because it was similar to Sinclair and she'd be less likely to make mistakes.

He shook her hand and flashed a blinding smile.

The skin at the corners of his astoundingly blue eyes crinkled. Deep dimples formed on both sides of his mouth. He peered closer to her veil. ''You look pretty good under there. Lucky me, I guess.''

She pulled her hand away. In all of her twenty-four years, she had never seen such a stunning man. His brilliant smile almost made her knees buckle.

Her earlier misgivings exploded into a ball of pure dread. Ryan obviously possessed the kind of innate male charm and incredible good looks that she'd sworn to avoid since a similarly handsome, seemingly charming man—Giorgio The Italian Scumbag—had taken off with a chunk of her heart a year ago.

She fell back a step, needing air and space and to think, and stumbled on her gown thanks to her shaky legs. Ryan quickly reached out and grasped her upper arm, steadying her with his warm, very large hand. Arrows of fire darted from his hand into her body and she barely managed to pull her arm from his hot touch.

Ryan moved closer and the scent of his aftershave washed over her. ''Hey, are you all right?''

*No, I'm not.* She'd never been able to keep her distance from handsome men, and, unfortunately had a history of making bad choices regarding them.

*History* being the key word.

Fighting the thoroughly ridiculous urge to lean closer and inhale more of his wonderful smell into her nose, Anna looked for an escape. She had no intention of exposing her real identity by posing for a fake wedding photo with a gorgeous man like Ryan. It was time to follow her instincts and do what she should have done when Colleen had suggested Anna fill in for the missing model an hour ago—run for her life, wedding dress and all. Thank goodness she hadn't signed the required photo release waiver yet.

She pointedly ignored Ryan and looked at Colleen. "I'm sorry, but I can't do this." She put herself into motion and marched across the grass in the general direction of the temporary dressing area on the upper level of the Rose Garden Park.

"Hey!" Ryan shouted. "Where are you going?"

"Anna!" Colleen called. "Wait…"

Anna ignored their calls, not wanting to deal with either of them. She didn't want *anyone* suspecting she wasn't simply Anna Simpson, humble bridal designer, struggling to make it on her own—without the benefit of the Sinclair name.

Before she had walked ten feet, she was jerked backward. Regaining her footing, she spun around. Ryan had placed a foot on the very edge of her dress's lacy train.

Pushy man. "Remove your foot, please," she said, her lips barely moving. "Do you have any idea how many hours went into the creation of this dress?" She'd spent months on this design, and had put blood, sweat and tears into the deceptively simple lace, satin, and pearl design. The beaded neckline alone had taken a professional seamstress three days to complete.

He shoved his cell phone into his pants pocket. "Look," he said, a shadow of contrition in his eyes. He bent and gently took the fragile Brussels lace of her train in his hand and pulled up the slack, effectively holding her in place while he pretended to brush it off. "I'm sorry for stepping on your dress. I just want to know why you're leaving. I thought we were supposed to have some pictures taken together."

He smiled again, showing teeth that looked as white as snow next to his lightly tanned face. "We'd make a great couple, don't you think?"

Her stomach flip-flopped at his smile.

*Oh, no, not again.*

She took a deep breath and tried to calm her racing nerves. She had no desire to be part of a couple with him, not even a pretend couple. After Giorgio, the last in a short but illustrious line of cheating, lying, beyond-handsome men, she didn't do "couple" anymore. She'd learned that what was on the inside of men was never as good as the outside looked. "Obviously I've changed my mind, Mr. Cavanaugh. Now would you please let go of my dress?"

"Oh, come on," he said softly, his face pulled into an appropriately serious expression. "Can't you just stay for one picture?"

Strangely, he seemed sincere, and his gentle tone caught her off guard. She slanted a glance up at him, reminding herself of how easy it would be for him to simply *pretend* to be sincere. "Look, I know I agreed to pose for these pictures, but I've changed my mind. I…uh, I didn't realize you were going to be my groom."

He swung his free arm wide with what looked like a forced smile on his lips. "What? I'm not good enough?"

*You're too good.* She managed a tremulous smile. "That's not it."

"Then what's the problem?" He leaned in close. "You did agree to this, didn't you?"

She stepped back, out of his scent's reach, and crossed her arms over her midriff, pressing the gown's delicate beading into her skin. He had a point.

She didn't want to leave Colleen without a bride any more than she wanted to sacrifice the media exposure and possible contract a photo of her dress in "The Bridal Chronicles" might bring.

But the *extra* media exposure that Ryan's good looks might bring frightened her for several reasons. Though it was silly, she detested having her picture taken; she'd been a gawky, unattractive child and had had too many unflattering pictures of her land on the front page of numerous publications. Also, she wanted to succeed as modest dress designer Anna Simpson, not heiress Anna Sinclair. Concealing her real identity was central to her plan.

And to succeed, she had to land the Perfect Bridal exclusive and make a profit. Then she would meet the requirements of the deal she and her father had made almost a year ago, within the time frame he'd decreed, which expired in less than a week. Then, she'd be able to follow her dream instead of working for her father at Sinclair Banking.

Wishing she possessed no sense of duty or fair play, she asked Ryan, "Why do you want me to do this shoot so badly?" She tried not to admire the absolute perfection of his chiseled face, heart-stopping sky-blue eyes, and full, sensual lips. And those dimples…

He lifted one broad shoulder. "Simple. I'm involved with a local charity's fund-raising campaign, and I'd like to raise awareness with as much publicity as I can."

A charity. Sounded like a worthwhile cause, one she wished she could help him with. But she couldn't. Hiding her face in one photo was feasible. More than one—she sincerely doubted it. There had to be another way. "Then why don't you just find another woman to be your bride?"

He bent close to her ear. "Oh, the answer to that is obvious," he whispered, his warm breath tickling her ear. "With a woman as beautiful as I'm certain you are, I bet we'd win Best Couple for sure. As a bonus, my charity is almost guaranteed lots of publicity."

A ribbon of hot excitement unfurled inside of her, joining a hard lump of guilt for letting him down. But she ignored the unsettling sensation and focused on what was important—her business, the one thing she could call her own, the one way she could show her true worth to the world—and her father. She didn't want to win Best Couple and be faced with more pictures.

Then again, she wasn't a heartless witch, either. She didn't want to be responsible for keeping his fund-raising efforts from garnering publicity. A giant arrow of guilt poked her.

She tried to move away from him, unable to think clearly with his big body looming over her, scrambling her senses and judgment like a banana in a blender.

Why did she always let attractive men keep her from thinking clearly? Had her sheltered childhood, spent at exclusive, all-girl boarding schools and under the close supervision of her autocratic, ultraconservative father warped her judgment? Had her lack of experience made her into a woman who perpetually made bad choices in the man department?

Maybe in the past. Not anymore.

Drawing a deep, cleansing breath, she wished she had the luxury of lapsing into a soothing session of meditation to calm her nerves. But she didn't. She would have to deal with Ryan without the benefit of her daily mantra.

"So," he said, letting out her train just enough to allow her to put some space between them. "How about being my bride?"

His "proposal" brought forth a familiar yearning. She had once dreamed of happily ever after with the man of her dreams. But now she had to be wary of men. She'd played the he-really-loves-me fool before and had fallen for attractive, charming men like him and had paid the price in heartache and tears. She didn't intend to make the same mistake one more time.

She'd finally acquired some sense.

She looked at Ryan again, liking the slightly humble expression on his face, even though she doubted it was real; charismatic men like Ryan usually got what they wanted without the need for humility. Even so, when Ryan threw her a small, hopeful smile, the foolish, appreciative, female side almost made her relent. And to her everlasting surprise, she found herself on the verge of giving him whatever he wanted.

On the verge, but not over the edge. Despite how guilty he was making her feel, probably deliberately, she just couldn't go through with this photo shoot. She had belatedly realized that being in the public eye wasn't someplace she could risk being. She might as well announce her true identity on the evening news, thereby sacrificing her "anonymous" identity.

Even though she still felt incredibly guilty that she couldn't help his charity, she said, "I'm sorry, Mr. Cavanaugh, but I've made up my mind. I have no intention of signing the photo-release waiver and allowing this photo to go to print." She looked pointedly down at the part of her dress he had in his arms, then clasped her hands together at her waist and gave him an imperious look. "Now please put my dress down. This photo shoot is over."

She'd have to find a way to live with her guilt and with disappointing him and Colleen, just as she would have to sacrifice the exposure "The Bridal Chronicles" would have given her design business. Not exactly what she'd planned.

But not appearing in the paper did have its upside. At least she wouldn't have to risk having her identity publicly unveiled, so to speak, and she certainly wouldn't have to live through some awful, unflattering picture gracing the cover of the newspaper.

Not much of an upside. The guilt alone would probably choke her. But it was the best she could do given the circumstances.

Fighting frustration, Ryan gripped Anna's dress, vaguely wondering what she looked like under that veil and why she was wearing the darn thing at all. Standing there, her hands clasped in front of her, the form-fitting, lacy dress she wore showing off her jaw-dropping curves, it was obvious she had a body for sin but was holding it like a schoolmarm.

Trying to ignore that sinful body, he focused instead on the question on his mind. Why was she so damned determined to run away from the shoot? Wouldn't it be good for her business?

Whatever the reason, there was no way he was going to let her walk out on their stint as pretend bride and groom. Keeping other kids from going through what he went through as a child, with nobody who gave a damn about them, was a long-standing goal. He wanted the publicity for the Mentor A Child Foundation and he wanted the media exposure to improve his tarnished reputation. He wasn't about to give up yet. He had to convince her to sign the release.

Time to appeal to her sensitive side.

"Can't you help me out here?" he asked. "It's just one photo, and you obviously intended to be part of this whole thing. It's no big deal, right?"

"Wrong." She tugged on her dress. "I changed my mind because it would be a big deal if we're chosen Best Wedding Couple. And with you in the photo, looking…so, well…*good,* we're virtually guaranteed to win."

Her compliment surprised him and lit a warm space inside of him; he still thought of himself as the scruffy, half-starved little kid from the wrong side of the tracks. "While I'm flattered, I was thinking we'd win because of you," he said, unable to squash the male curiosity that made him want to get a clear look at her face through her veil.

"You can flatter and charm me all you want, but I'm still not going to risk winning Best Couple."

He frowned. "Isn't winning good?"

"Not always. I…well, I just don't want the attention, all right?"

He held up a hand. "But we're only talking a few pictures in wedding clothes—"

"Which will turn into more pictures and interviews and attention I don't want." She shook her head. "Please try to understand."

*Damn.* He'd assumed she was game for the shoot since she was here, decked out in full bride gear. Obviously, for some reason, that wasn't the case.

Contingency plan. Time to change her mind.

He touched the tip of her creamy shoulder, exposed by her off-the-shoulder gown. "Are you sure you won't reconsider?" he said, unable to help lingering on her smooth, warm skin. Did she have the face to go with her flawless complexion and stunning body, perfectly shown off by the pretty, figure-hugging dress she wore? "Lots of needy little kids will benefit." Needy little kids like he'd once been.

She tugged on her dress, inadvertently touching his hand in the process. "I feel bad enough as it is, so please don't try to guilt me into helping you out. Would you please let me go?"

Heat flared in his body and he tried to ignore how the mere touch of her hand almost knocked the wind out of him. Damn, he wanted to lift that filmy veil and see what she really looked like. Sweat broke out on his upper lip.

*Get a hold of yourself and focus.*

He was counting on the media exposure for Mentor A Child this chronicle thing would generate. He couldn't afford to let his obvious attraction to Anna distract him and keep him from attaining that goal, or from counteracting the recent spate of image-bashing publicity his former employee Joanna's personal vendetta had caused. Damage he needed to repair before the Mentor A Child Board of Directors decided he wasn't the kind of guy they wanted connected to their organization.

For the sake of the foundation, he had to find a way to make this work, to help needy kids who didn't have a loving adult in their lives and would fall through the cracks if the foundation wasn't around to help them.

Like he had.

One way or another, he'd convince Anna to sign that release.

Luckily he was very good at getting what he wanted.

Her jaw set, Anna watched Ryan fiddle with the lace-edged train of her dress, wishing he'd let her go and leave her alone. "I'll say it again, Mr. Cavanaugh. Please let go of my dress."

He looked at her with those compelling blue eyes, a speculative expression on his face. He inclined his head. "Of course." He let go of her train and smoothed it out. "Your tail thing is ready. I'll walk you to the dressing tent." He walked toward the makeshift changing area, a crease marring his tanned brow.

Relieved, but wary of his sudden turnabout, she fell in step beside him, ridiculously marveling at his strong, masculine profile. "I'm sorry I can't help you out—" Without warning, her head jerked backward. "Hey!" She spun around and caught her shoe on an uneven patch of grass and teetered on the backs of her heels, her arms flailing.

Before she could find her balance, she fell sideways. Her veil, attached to her head with small combs, ripped off, jerking her head back again. She crashed to the ground like a felled tree, landing half on her rear, half on her back with a *clump* next to another thorn-encrusted rosebush, her gown poofing up around her like a giant marshmallow.

Her breath whooshed out of her and it took a moment to regain her wits. She slowly sat up, shaking her veil-less head, then looked up and saw Ryan peering down at her, his face creased with concern.

"Hey, are you all right?" He held out a hand. "That was some fall."

She grabbed his hand, ignoring how warm and strong it felt, and pulled herself up, searching for her veil. She just wanted to escape before anyone recognized her. She could see the headline now:

Heiress Anna Sinclair Turns Her Back On Millions, Pretending To Be Bridal Designer

Some terribly unflattering photo of her flopped on the grass of the Rose Garden would undoubtedly accompany the headline....

She suppressed a tremor of disgust.

When she was standing, her legs still wobbly, Ryan stepped closer and slid his arm around her shoulders. "Are you sure you're all right?"

His masculine scent washed over her, an intoxicating combination of clean male and expensive designer aftershave, and a ribbon of attraction darted through her. She swiveled her head and stared into his gaze, unable to find her sanity and look away, tumbling into the clear, compelling depths of his eyes. Awareness crashed through her like a tidal wave and she wanted to reach out and run her fingers over the sheer beauty of his strong jaw. A light breeze stirred, mixing his scent with the heady fragrance of freshly bloomed roses.

A couple of clicks sounded.

She instinctively cringed and snapped her gaze toward the sound.

"Thanks, guys." A photographer triumphantly

held up his camera. "One of those is sure to be a keeper."

Panic seeped through her. Her worst fantasy had come true. Some overzealous photographer had taken a photo of her without her veil! "He just took our picture!"

Ryan stepped away and plucked her veil free from the rosebush it had snagged on. "Yeah, I guess he did." A tiny smile hovered around his mouth.

She crossed her arms in front of her, wanting to wipe that little smirk off his face with everything in her. "You're happy about this, aren't you?"

"Hey, I wanted the picture taken all along, and you don't seem willing to tell me why you're so darned determined to back out."

The despicable schemer. Had he arranged for the photographer to snap the picture on the sly?

She drew herself up and did her best to look haughty. "Well, Mr. Cavanaugh, the picture may have been taken, but I still haven't signed the release." She hastily gathered her dress, snatched her tulle veil from his hand, and stomped away. "And I don't intend to," she called over her shoulder.

"Not even for a worthwhile cause?"

She stopped and shot him a glare. "I'll say it again. Don't use guilt to change my mind, Mr. Cavanaugh. Trust me, guilt isn't in short supply today." She turned her back on the gorgeous man with the charming dimples, bone-melting smile, and enough charisma to raise a hundred red flags in her brain.

Thankfully, this ended here and now. She wasn't about to let her one lapse in judgment, or Ryan's attempt to make her feel guilty, ruin her plan to meet the terms of her father's deal so she wouldn't have to slave away in the family banking business.

She shuddered. Even though she possessed the skill and education to help run a banking dynasty, she couldn't think of anything worse than being relegated to the uncreative, stodgy world of high finance for the rest of her life.

Her father's world.

That was enough to keep her walking. She set her shoulders, needing to get away from the exasperating man with the gorgeous blue eyes, stunning smile, and his compelling reason to make sure the picture *was* printed.

Even though it went against her natural sense of fair play and altruism not to help him out, she had to ignore the guilt ripping through her and stand firm. Her future, her happiness, her self-worth were at stake. That picture would never see the light of day. Ryan would just have to get his publicity some other way, and she knew from experience that that was do-able.

After all of the schemers who had betrayed and used her, she was done serving any man's purpose.

## Chapter Two

Ryan watched Anna clomp across the grass, her dress held high and her chin shoved into the air. A hearty dose of admiration overrode the puzzled irritation caused by her refusal to stay for the shoot. Most people saw him as a formidable foe and got the hell out of the way when he wanted something. She obviously had no problem crossing him. She was something else, all right, with her sassy threats and mule-headed refusal to cooperate.

He liked that. She was up-front and to-the-point.

Unlike any of the other women he'd known.

A vision of Sonya, the rich man-eater who'd burned him, thudded into his head. He'd met her through a mutual friend, and they'd hit it off right away. Quickly becoming inseparable, they'd become engaged after six months. He'd been happy and confident of their future, and had been totally unprepared for her calling off the wedding a month before the date. Apparently she'd determined—with quite a bit of help from her snooty parents—that despite his recent business success, he wasn't rich enough for her taste. She'd left him almost standing at the altar, and had married a "trust funder" like her a week after she was supposed to marry Ryan.

Her cutting, unexpected betrayal had left him shell-shocked, hurt and pretty damn determined to avoid her kind—wealthy princesses who chewed up and spit out men they deemed unworthy.

But this Anna, well, she seemed to be a hardworking girl and nothing like the heiress who'd dumped him on his butt. Not that her being down-to-earth and normal really mattered. What did matter was that he wanted to keep needy little kids from having the kind of lonely, neglected childhood he'd had. He wanted the publicity for the foundation. Unfortunately it looked like Anna wasn't going to help him out and sign that release.

And that was really a shame. If any woman could help him win Best Wedding Couple, she could. Man, what a beauty she was, all fiery auburn hair, big, gorgeous brown eyes the color of aged brandy, and smooth, pale skin. He'd need to start being solicitous, something he wished he'd thought of earlier. He impatiently unbuttoned his coat and loosened his bow tie, still feeling warm.

He *had* to convince her to help him out.

He stared at the tent for a second, his mind firing up. How could he change her mind to his way of thinking? Maybe he could turn her around if he knew what he was up against.

Maybe not.

Either way, now that the picture had been taken, he would do his best to make sure the paper published it. It was time to make use of his well-developed sales skills, honed from having to battle for every inch of his business success, to make Anna see the light.

A nice, conciliatory lunch seemed in order.

He headed toward the dressing tents, consisting of temporary rooms created by draped black fabric and wood frames. Anna was nowhere in sight, but he figured she was still changing, unless she'd taken off in full wedding attire.

He moved closer to the opening in the fluttering material, spying the reporter—was her name Colleen?—as he drew near. The tall, attractive blonde stepped out, looking as frustrated as he felt.

"She still changing?" he asked.

She nodded and gave a tiny roll of her blue eyes. "She's pretty mad."

"I know." He loosened his tie more, which was beginning to strangle the life out of him.

She gave him a wry smile. "You must have really gotten under her skin."

Before he could react to that regrettable assessment, Anna's head popped out from between the sheets. "I can hear every word you're saying, you know."

He stared at her for a long second, knocked speechless again by her lush auburn hair, clear, stunning brown eyes, arched eyebrows and creamy, flawless skin.

What a looker.

Recovering, he gave her a lopsided grin and winked, determined to keep things light. Maybe humor would gain her cooperation. "Then we'll have to save any secrets for later."

She wrinkled her nose at him. "How can you joke around?"

He shrugged. "Maybe we both need to lighten up."

She looked at the reporter. "Can't you get rid of him?"

The other woman backed away, waving her hands in front of her. "I'm not getting involved in any of this." She took her keys out of her purse. "I gotta go."

"Traitor," Anna said under her breath, her face screwed into a frown.

The reporter laughed. "Hey, I'm not helping either one of you out." She raised a brow. "You backed out on our deal, so you're on your own, although I would like you to reconsider and sign the release. Think how good it would be for your business."

Anna's scowl faded, but the tiny crease between her brows remained. "I'm really sorry, Colleen. I lost my nerve."

"I know. But my editor is expecting to go ahead with the whole thing, especially since you're the last photo to be taken and the spread's almost ready for production." She turned to leave. "Why don't you think about it and contact me later, all right?" she said over her shoulder. "And keep in mind how hard it will be for me to find someone else on such short notice."

Anna half nodded and Colleen left. Ryan mulled over how Joe Capriati, the supervising editor, had stressed the importance of the photo-release waiver. According to Joe, the *Beacon* required the release because some woman had sued the paper after they'd printed her picture without her permission the year before. They weren't taking any chances now.

He looked to Anna, gearing up to do a little steamrolling to convince her to change her mind and sign that release.

She had pressed her glossy, pink lips into a firm line and was glaring at him, something he didn't get the impression she did very often.

"Please leave me alone," she said.

He raised his brows. "Oooooh, that's real scary."

She sniffed and yanked her head back into the dressing room, rattling the curtain. "I can be scarier, I assure you."

His smile grew. Even though she could blow his whole plan for damage control and good publicity for the foundation sky-high, he liked her gumption. "Yeah, you're a real scary gal," he said, searching for levity.

He then took out his handheld, electronic planner and consulted it. No meetings until four o'clock. Plenty of time to convince her to sign the release. "How about lunch?"

She popped her head out and blinked owlishly. "You're asking me out?"

"Well, yeah. Is that a problem?"

"Maybe." She disappeared again. A moment later, she emerged wearing a light pink cotton sweater and figure-hugging, dark blue designer jeans that showed off her trim but curvy body. She had her wedding dress, covered by a garment bag, draped over one arm and an oversized straw tote bag in the other hand.

He snagged another look at her curves without being too obvious, his blood percolating. Damn, she was hot.

"I don't usually go out with guys like you," she said.

Guys like him. His hackles raised. Could she somehow smell the dirt poor of his childhood on him? He was sure that was one of the reasons Sonya had dumped him.

He crossed his arms over his chest. "What do you mean, 'like me'?"

"You know." She waved a hand in the air. "Good-looking. Dimpled. Don't make me go on."

His hackles relaxed and her compliment filled him with a sense of pleasure. "Oh, so you'd rather spend time with an unappealing man without dimples?"

"Quite frankly, yes." She ran her hands through her heavily styled, dark red hair, loosening the stiff strands. "I've found that most really charismatic men are selfish, manipulative, and—" she shrugged "—hurtful."

Ryan instantly wanted to know what selfish jerk had hurt her. But he was pretty sure she wouldn't share that sort of information with him. She barely knew him. "How about if I promise to behave? Then will you go? Quite frankly, I'm starving." And he hated that feeling. It reminded him how often he hadn't had enough to eat during his childhood. Now, eating was his favorite pastime.

She sighed heavily and crossed her arms over her chest.

"Look," he said, taking another tack to convince her to go. "What's the harm in an innocent lunch? You have to eat, right?"

She looked at him, an odd worry clearly reflected in her brown eyes. She chewed on her lip, glanced away, then looked back. She then rummaged around in her tote bag. "Can we go somewhere vegetarian?"

He cringed. He'd been a meat and potatoes man, and whatever else he could get his hands on, after he'd spent his childhood living off nothing but his mom's stale sandwiches made with a layer of peanut butter so thin he could barely taste it. "How about a compromise?" he suggested. "I know a place where you can go veggie and I can get a thick steak."

She drew out a large pair of dark sunglasses and put them on. "You eat steak? For lunch? That sounds wonderful."

He stared quizzically at the shades for a moment. Why was she wearing such big, ugly sunglasses? He then cupped her elbow with his hand, appreciating the softness of her skin. "You don't look like you need to diet." Not with a body like that. And it surprised him that she liked the sound of steak. He figured her for a genuine legumes-for-lunch kind of gal.

"I don't, but in the interest of keeping my body healthy, I make myself stay away from fatty food," she said. She pierced him with her dark eyes. "Okay. You've talked me into it. Lead the way."

"Let me change and we'll go." He headed toward the tent where he'd left his street clothes, inordinately happy she'd agreed to go considering this lunch was nothing but an opportunity to convince her to sign the release.

As he changed out of his tux, a vision of Sonya rose in his brain like a bad dream. Maybe he shouldn't spend any time with Anna, who he was obviously attracted to.

He willed away the tiny lump of anxiety taking up residence in his gut. *Relax.* Lunch with Anna was no big deal. It was for his image and his pet charity, an organization that helped underprivileged kids. Two very good causes he was committed to. Yes, lunch with the delectable Anna was simply a casual meal designed to garner her cooperation.

Nothing more than that, right?

Anna followed the waiter through the posh restaurant to their table. She tried to calm her still fluttering nerves. What had possessed her to agree to this lunch?

Aside from her unacceptable fascination with the handsome man following behind her, his hand burning a hole in the small of her back, of course.

Actually, she'd agreed to appease her guilt, hoping she could help Ryan come up with another way to acquire the publicity he wanted for his charity. She'd had quite a bit of experience, through her mother, with charitable organizations and fund-raising.

And it certainly wasn't a crime to enjoy a necessary meal with an attractive, charming male, something she hadn't experienced since Giorgio had swept her off her feet.

A cold shiver slid up her spine. Giorgio had been oh-so-attractive and charming at first, blinding her to his true nature and intentions. Like a total ninny, she'd forgotten all of the other men who'd burned her and she'd fallen for him faster than a bear stock market. She couldn't let down her guard and make that mistake again.

Thankfully, this was a simple lunch to discuss Ryan's charity, not a date. Forcing her thoughts away from Giorgio, she swallowed and tried to focus on her goal—to find another way to help Ryan so he would leave her alone, ensuring her secret identity would be safe.

She pressed her large straw hat lower on her head and adjusted her sunglasses when every woman they passed turned to watch Ryan walk by. At what she guessed to be well over six feet two inches, he was hard to miss. Especially since his tall, broad body was impeccably presented by the well-cut designer business suit he'd changed into. He moved with an easy, loose-limbed male grace that all women probably found hard to ignore.

Anna vowed to fly in the face of tradition.

Ryan was just a guy who had offered to buy her lunch.

No problem.

She would simply eat lunch, brainstorm about fund-raising, and that would be the end of their brief association.

The waiter seated them in a secluded booth at a table draped in white linen, set with lots of crystal and silver gleaming in the muted afternoon sunlight. People dressed in business attire talked in subdued tones and muted strains of Vivaldi floated to her ears.

The pleasant, earthy scent of cooking meat laced the air. Her mouth watered but she tried to ignore the feeling in favor of maintaining a healthy diet.

Did Ryan eat at such elegant places often? She usually avoided swanky restaurants because she'd spent too many hours of her youth stuck with the pretensions and dictates of society her father had drilled into her head.

She could make her own choices now, thank goodness.

Anna took the menu and opened it, pleased and

surprised by the vegetarian selections, then glanced at Ryan. "Aren't you going to look at the menu?"

"I already know what I'm having."

"Oh. So you come here often?"

"All the time. Their steaks are the best in town."

"You like to eat, don't you?" she asked, smiling.

A shadow appeared in his eyes. "Yeah, I do," he said curtly.

She drew her brows together, puzzled by his clipped answer, then turned her attention back to the menu. Even though her mouth was still watering over the smell of steak in the air, she suppressed a shudder at what his arteries must look like if he ate red meat all the time.

She then decided on a pasta and vegetable dish, and looked back at Ryan, who gazed at her with undisguised interest. "What?" she asked, ignoring the thrill that raced through her when he looked at her with his piercing blue eyes.

He kicked up the corner of his mouth. "I was just wondering why you're wearing that hat and glasses. They don't look like your style."

She glanced away, then pushed her hair behind her ear beneath her hat. How could she possibly explain her outlandish disguise? The truth was, she couldn't without giving away her real identity.

But Ryan had already seen her face, and hadn't recognized her. Maybe her auburn dye job had thrown him off track. Since their booth was fairly well hidden, perhaps she could dispense with the hat and glasses during lunch to shove Ryan off the subject. "I...uh, well..." She removed her hat and glasses and put them in her straw tote bag. "No reason." She gave him a brilliant smile.

He stared at her appreciatively and smiled back, shaking his head as if so say, "Yeah, right." "Okay, you have your reasons, which you obviously aren't going to share with me. What I want to know is why you agreed to pose for the spread in the first place."

She held up her hands. "Look, I know it seems strange, but the regular model didn't show and I needed my gown to be part of the spread." She picked up her water glass and gave him a wry smile. "I know changing my mind might seem silly. But when you showed up…well, you weren't what I was expecting."

He leaned his forearms on the table and lifted a quizzical brow. "How so?"

"Oh, come on," she said, smiling. "You must know that you're an attractive man. I didn't want to risk winning Best Couple and having to take part in any more…stuff." Being in front of a camera had always terrified her. Or, rather, the results terrified her.

"Oh, so I'm a dangerous guy, then?" he asked, mischief glinting in his eyes. His dimple flashed at the corner of his mouth. "I'm wounded."

Anna felt herself heating up, reacting to his teasing tone and appealing, lazy grin. "Yeah, I'll bet." She took a long swig of water, hoping to cool down. "You, Mr. Cavanaugh, are the kind of man who is inherently dangerous."

His expression sobered. "You're serious."

"Absolutely. I've known men like you." Men who made you trust, convinced you to believe, then broke your heart. "All flash and charisma. Nothing more."

He leaned forward, his eyes intent. "Thanks a lot. And maybe I should mention that the wedding pictures were going to be fake, remember? You weren't really marrying me, you know.''

No, she wasn't. She was never going to have the kind of fairy-tale wedding she designed gowns for. She doubted she'd ever be marrying anyone or that she would ever be able to trust another man again. And that had to be fine. If she succeeded in meeting her father's terms, her design business would be enough and, more importantly, would prove she had worth beyond her cash value or her banking skills.

She inclined her head. ''You have a point, and I realize I may have…overreacted. But in my opinion, with you as my groom, winning Best Couple would have been a given.''

He glanced down and almost looked embarrassed by her compliment. ''Well, I don't know about that…'' He trailed off and cleared his throat. ''So you think you overreacted?'' he asked, blatantly directing the subject away from himself.

She took a whole wheat roll from the basket on the table and eyed Ryan thoughtfully, wondering about the incongruity between his extreme good looks and polish and his almost blushing discomfiture over her flattering remark. ''Maybe,'' she hedged, hardly able to tell him that what other men had put her through had left a wound that affected all of the decisions she made. ''Why all the questions?''

He rubbed his neck and looked sideways at her. ''Other than the fact that you're running around like a secret agent with a floppy hat and dark glasses on?'' He opened one side of his jacket, cocked his head toward his shoulder and said, ''Come in Double-O-Seven, come in.''

She grinned and held up her hands, liking this teasing, lighthearted side of him. "All right, all right," she said, laughing. "I get the picture." She sat for a long moment, gradually sobering. She had to remember why her disguise was so important—she wanted to succeed on her own. "I admit, what I'm doing seems strange, and maybe a little comical, but, trust me, I have a good reason, all right?"

He gazed at her for a moment, his expression turning serious, then nodded. "All right. And for the record, I was also asking questions because I'm curious about why you backed out. As I said, my charity is in the middle of a fund-raising campaign, and could really use the publicity the article would have generated. Seeing as how the Mentor A Child Foundation will suffer, I wanted to know what your reasons were."

A bothersome sensation rolled around inside of her. Mentor A Child helped little kids and she might be keeping that from happening. "Are my admittedly nebulous reasons good enough for you?"

He lifted a shoulder in a half shrug. "I guess, although I was hoping maybe you'd reconsider."

A heavy load of guilt for not helping him smothered her. "Isn't there any other way to get the publicity you need?" she asked, hoping to appease her guilt. She'd always been a pleaser, just like her mom, and it went against her natural instincts to do something that might hurt someone else—especially needy children.

"Maybe. But this article would reach a lot of readers and would be a great way to raise awareness for the Mentor A Child Foundation." He paused and took a roll and put it on his bread plate. "Although there is a bungee-jumping stunt I was considering."

Horror shot through her. "Bungee jumping? Are you crazy?"

"No, just driven to support this charity," he said seriously. "Mentor A Child helps little kids who have nobody else in their lives."

She was surprised that a flashy guy like him would care about little kids. Most didn't. "Why don't you just pay to run ads on TV or in the newspaper then? I'm sure you could afford to do that, right?"

He looked away. "I could," he said, inclining his head, a new shadow lurking in his eyes. "And I will if I have to. But…this way the publicity wouldn't seem so self-serving. You know what I mean?"

She nodded, studying him, sensing that there was more to this than he was letting on. But she wouldn't press; she had her little secret, too, and the less said, the better.

The waiter arrived. Anna ordered, knowing she needed to eat, but the guilt and apprehension roiling around in her stomach like acid had killed her appetite. Was she overreacting and being selfish by saying no to the article? Or was she just being smart by keeping her distance from a man who seemed so much like the other men who'd scorched her, not to mention that she would be ensuring the success of her business? She'd never had something that she could call her own, something that wasn't somehow given to her because of her connection to the Sinclair name. It was important for her dream to succeed on her own merits.

On the other hand, it was exceedingly difficult to ignore the fact that she was disappointing a lot of people, and possibly damaging Ryan's charity, by backing out now. Should she reconsider? It had always been tough for her to put herself first, to stand up to other people, usually her dad, to get what she wanted.

Feeling torn, she eyed Ryan. "I feel really bad about all of this."

He pinned her with his sapphire eyes. "Bad enough to change your mind?"

She let out a heavy breath. How had this become so complicated? Ever since she'd attended a fairy-tale wedding when she was a young girl, all she'd ever wanted to do was design wedding dresses. The fantasy of weddings had always appealed to her. To be able to do that, however, she had to meet her father's terms, and that meant concealing her identity long enough to succeed on her own.

It didn't help that, just like her dear mother, Anna had a soft streak a mile wide and a deep sense of altruism she was proud of. Her mother had always supported numerous charities.

Thinking of her wonderfully philanthropic mother clinched it. Anna simply couldn't, in good conscience, ignore his charitable efforts. "Oh, all right," she whispered, gripping the edge of the table, hoping she didn't regret this decision. "I'll sign the release."

He reached over and put his hand on hers, then gently rubbed his fingers over the back of her hand. The contact made her jump, but she didn't retract her hand. Warmth spread into every cell in her body, and she wanted to curl her fingers around his big, solid hand. She didn't. Ryan was the wrong man for her to hold on to. She knew now that any man was.

"Thank you," he said, his eyes warm with gratitude. "I appreciate it."

She tugged her hand from his, needing to sever the connection between them. She might have overreacted to "The Bridal Chronicles," but she wasn't overreacting to Ryan. He was dangerous, everything she'd learned to avoid.

She reached for her water glass again and gulped some down. When she'd arrived at the restaurant, she hadn't thought having lunch with Ryan would be a problem. But she'd been dead wrong. Not only had he talked her into signing the release, but she was also extremely attracted to a man she should stay away from.

Was history repeating itself?

A hollow pit formed in her stomach and she couldn't help feeling that she was making another giant mistake.

Ryan stood next to his car and put up a hand to Anna as she climbed into her small car. She'd promised to meet him at the *Beacon* right away to sign the release.

Dragging his eyes away from the enticing curve of her hip as she slid into the seat, he focused on her gorgeous face, the lower part visible beneath the wide brim of the ridiculous hat she'd put back on.

What a beauty she was. He'd been spellbound by her creamy skin and how it had glowed in the muted lighting of the restaurant. Her thick, dark red hair had perfectly contrasted with her porcelain complexion and stunning, amber-shaded eyes.

Yeah, she was just the "bride" he needed. He frowned. For publicity, of course. After Sonya's torching, posing for a fake wedding photo was as close as he'd ever get to being part of a wedded couple.

He sat down, turned on the ignition, and shifted his Porsche into gear, heading out of the parking lot.

Thank goodness his lunch date had turned out so well and Anna had changed her mind.

As he cruised toward the bridge that would take him over the Willamette River, he relaxed. Anna had agreed to sign the release, clearing the way for the picture to be printed. The Mentor A Child Foundation would get the publicity they needed and, hopefully, lots of neglected kids would be spared the kind of childhood he'd had. No thanks to Joanna, his image was well on the way to being squeaky clean again.

Smiling, he downshifted and zipped past another car, enjoying the sight of the Portland skyline, rising majestically in front of him against the spectacular, blue summer sky. He glanced down at the river running beneath the bridge. Sailboats and pleasure-craft bobbed like toys on the sparkling water. Casting his gaze right, he admired the other bridges connecting Portland's east and west sides. Ahead of him loomed the West Hills, studded with evergreens glowing like emeralds in the sun.

Light-years from the ramshackle dump located in a podunk town in eastern Washington State he'd grown up in. Surrounded by poverty, constantly hungry, he'd dreamed of living in a city like Portland, a prosperous city full of tall buildings, sparkling rivers and opportunities for those, like himself, willing to work for them.

With those dreams driving him, he'd left his dirt-poor, horrific childhood and neglectful parents behind at seventeen. He'd worked his way through college digging ditches, scraped his way up and built his business from nothing. Now, ten years after he'd graduated, he was a successful businessman. He had the opportunity to promote an organization he believed in, an organization that helped kids who reminded him of himself.

When he reached the west side of the river, he swung a quick left and headed toward the office of the *Beacon.* Heady anticipation rose in him, carving away some of the worry that had been eating at him since Joanna had dumped her lies on the press about the kind of employer he was and his image had taken a nosedive, threatening his involvement with the foundation.

Tightening his hand on the steering wheel, he downshifted and jetted through an intersection, just making the light. He stopped at the next red light, looked in the rearview mirror and straightened his tie. Best Wedding Couple and free publicity for the Mentor A Child Foundation were just around the corner. Things were going exactly the way he wanted.

Within days, his problems would be solved.

And Anna's problems?

Ryan shoved that niggling thought away. Anna might be a hardworking, normal woman he admired, but that didn't make any difference. He needed to concentrate on what was important.

His business.

His charity work.

Keeping his heart safe.

After Sonya, he couldn't let anything else matter.

# *Chapter Three*

After she met Ryan at the *Beacon* and signed the release, Anna had her long-awaited meeting with Mr. Lewis, the president of Perfect Bridal. He'd seemed impressed with her designs, but admitted he was concerned about her lack of design credentials and virtually unknown name. She left the meeting with his promise to contact her in a few days when he'd made a decision about which designer he would feature exclusively in his stores.

Feeling deflated, and a bit desperate, she'd headed back to her hotel, thankful the meeting hadn't been a total disaster. Mr. Lewis hadn't recognized her, something she always worried about when she wasn't able to wear her disguise during business meetings.

As she'd driven to her hotel after dropping her soiled wedding gown at the dry cleaners, she had decided that the decision she'd made to sign the release and let the picture go to print had been the right one, for both her and Ryan. If Mr. Lewis saw the picture in print, he might view her as more established and be more inclined to choose her designs. Ryan's charity would benefit. It seemed like a win-win situation.

The next day, she spent most of her time in her hotel room, working a new design that featured lots of taffeta and delicate Italian lace, then munching on the healthiest snacks she could find in the hotel vending machine. As she worked, concentrating on the square neckline and bell-shaped sleeves, she ignored thoughts of Ryan clamoring through her brain, absolutely determined *not* to remember how his hair had looked like dark honey in the sunlight. How his tux had hugged his well-honed physique. How his electric-blue eyes had zeroed in on her, making her pulse speed up.

She drummed her drawing pencil on the table, her lip clamped between her teeth, looking at her sketch. She raised a brow. The clean lines, defined by the taffeta skirt, looked right, and the overall medieval look appealed to her, but the empire waist and the dimensions of the neckline, which she'd been working on for an hour, were off.

Frustrated, she tore off the page to expose a clean sheet of paper. Blue eyes appeared in her brain…

Darn. Why was she unable to get Ryan out of her mind?

She dropped the pencil and fidgeted. She then scraped her thumbnail clean of the French manicure nail polish that she'd painstakingly applied last night while watching old *Brady Bunch* reruns on TV, fantasizing about growing up in the Brady's normal—or her skewed perception of normal—household.

Her phone rang and she jumped. Ryan? Eyeing the

phone, she chided herself for thinking he had any reason to call her and snatched the handset up. "Hello?"

"Miss Simpson?"

"Yes?"

"This is the concierge desk. Pierre's Dry Cleaning is here to deliver your cleaning, but there's a bit of a problem. Would you mind coming down to clear this up?"

She breathed a sigh of relief that it wasn't Ryan, only to suffer a spurt of anxiety over the wedding dress. "I'll be right down."

A few minutes later, she hurried across the lobby to the concierge desk. The dress was one of only a few she'd brought with her. It was made of lots of delicate satin, fragile lace and intricate beadwork, and the matching veil was fragile, as well. She fervently hoped the dry cleaners hadn't ruined or misplaced it. "I'm Miss Simpson. You have my dry cleaning?"

The older, gray-haired man behind the desk smiled. "Ah, yes, miss. Thank you for coming down." He held up the large dry cleaning parcel, then pointed to the receipt. "As you can see, the receipt from Pierre's clearly stated you had left two items, yet only one item was returned."

She nodded, frowning slightly. "Yes, I did leave two items." She unzipped the heavy plastic garment bag. "A dress and a veil." She carefully moved the bead-encrusted dress aside and let out a breath when she spied the spidery veil tucked inside. "And they're both here."

"Ah, good. Just wanted to be sure." He motioned for a young man, presumably from Pierre's, to come forward. "Everything is in order."

The short, blond young man looked at her,

squinted, then pointed to her face. "Hey, I know you. Aren't you from Philly?" He cocked his head to the side and squinted. "Aren't you some rich dude's daughter? I used to live there, and my girlfriend cut out newspaper pictures of you and taped them all over the place, trying to get her hair to look like yours." He shook his head, smiling appreciatively. "Man, she never even came close. Didn't you used to be a brunette?"

A chill skipped up Anna's spine. She reached up to her head. Darn. She'd left her room in such a hurry she'd forgotten her hat and glasses.

He continued staring, then snapped his fingers. "Anna Sinclair, right?"

Her stomach twisted into a panic-induced knot, she ducked her head, grabbed her dry cleaning and mumbled, "Must be somebody else." She took off at a sharp clip across the lobby, wondering how she could have been so stupid as to forget her hat and glasses.

One quick trip to the lobby without her disguise and some dry cleaner deliveryman had recognized her. Granted, he was from Philadelphia, and she was much less well-known here in Oregon. But his recognizing her still bothered her.

While she waited for the elevator, chewing on her lip in the unladylike way her father hated, one thought blazed through her brain. She absolutely couldn't afford to risk her identity and a chance to realize her dream, as Anna Simpson, by allowing the picture of her and Ryan go to print, even if Mr. Lewis might view the extra publicity as positive.

Even if she felt incredibly bad that she couldn't help Ryan's charity.

Oh, how she wished she'd put this all together *be-*

*fore* she foolishly agreed to fill in for the missing model.

Before she'd lost all of her backbone and signed the release.

Luckily she'd come to her senses before the picture was everywhere. Surely she could simply unsign the release.

As she rode in the elevator back to her room, thankfully alone, she made a conscious effort to relax and not feel so badly about putting her needs first. Even though she felt enormously guilty that Ryan's charity would suffer, he would just have to understand what was important to her.

She would do almost anything to make her dream come true.

And while Ryan *might* understand that, she somehow doubted a determined man like him would be happy things weren't going to go his way.

Anna tapped her foot in the mahogany-trimmed, mirrored elevator whisking her up to Ryan's office and adjusted her dark glasses. She'd called to be sure he'd be here and then she'd followed his instructions and driven to his office to deliver the news that she'd changed her mind in person. It was the least she could do considering things weren't going to turn out the way he wanted after all.

Unfortunately that couldn't be helped. That deliveryman recognizing her had been a huge wake-up call, a giant reminder of how important it was that she keep her identity a secret and succeed on her own.

She stepped off the elevator, settled her floppy hat down on her head, looked up—and froze. Ryan was heading toward her, moving with the innate male grace she had noticed yesterday. He looked simply gorgeous.

Her heartbeat fluttered like a hummingbird's.

The dark brown designer suit he wore accentuated the honey tones in his hair and contrasted vividly with his clear blue eyes. The cut was ideal on his wide-shouldered, muscular body, and the green, blue and gold patterned tie he wore, which would look gaudy on any other man, worked quite well on him and completed the thoroughly masculine package flawlessly.

He smiled at her and his dimples appeared. She yanked her gaze from him, focusing instead on the gigantic fresh floral bouquets, gold-framed, original artwork and chic taupe leather couches in the lobby. She kept walking toward him, even though her legs felt like rubber. She would not let his good looks and bone-melting smile weaken her resolve to prove to her father she could make a success of her business. After today, she and Ryan would have no reason to ever see each other again.

Anna smiled shakily and took his outstretched hand. His fingers surrounded hers, wrapping her hand in a deep warmth that seeped into the rest of her body like sunshine on a hot summer day.

"Nice to see you again, Double-O-Seven," he said, a teasing glint in his eyes, slowly letting her hand slide from his. "Shall we step into my office?"

Her heart pulsed, expanding and contracting in an odd way. She nodded and followed him down a long, maple-paneled corridor. The sooner she delivered her news and escaped from him, the better.

He pushed open a large, glossy wooden door and motioned for her to enter. She stepped by him and looked around the spacious office. One wall, lined with floor-to-ceiling windows, provided a spectacular view of the city of Portland. Taupe designer drapes framed those incredible windows and a huge, mahogany desk, matching credenza and large leather chair sat directly opposite the door. The desktop was bare except for an open laptop computer, a marble penholder and a gold clock.

A gleaming personal gym occupied the other side of the room, explaining Ryan's great body. A dark leather couch and loveseat sat on the left, arranged around a brass and marble coffee table topped with a fresh flower arrangement. Built-in mahogany bookcases, filled with books and magazines, lined the wall behind the couch. Original, abstract artwork adorned the grass-cloth walls.

He moved toward the couch and she followed, trying to control the strange, frantic beating of her heart. She was simply nervous about delivering the bad news, that was all.

He turned and indicated the love seat with his hand. "Have a seat. Can I get you anything to drink?"

She shook her head and gave in to her shaking knees and sat, sure she was too nervous to choke down any kind of liquid.

Ryan unbuttoned his suit coat and lowered his big body onto the couch. "So. What can I do for you?" A slight crease marred the space between his tawny eyebrows.

She shifted uneasily and removed her hat and sunglasses. "Uh…well…" She cleared her throat and avoided looking directly at him, apprehensive about disappointing him. Would he get angry and yell like her father always did when she wouldn't do what he wanted?

She made a conscious effort to relax. "I…I've decided I don't want our photo printed."

"What?" He shook his head, his face pressed into a frown. Rising, he looked at her, then swung around, pacing. "Obviously something's bothering you. Why is it so important to keep the picture from going to print?"

She chewed on her lip, rationalizing that she probably *did* owe him some sort of explanation since she'd signed the release. But she couldn't give him the *real* explanation without exposing who she really was. Maybe she could give him an abridged version, leaving out any details related to her identity.

She cleared her throat. "My father expects me to join the family business in Philadelphia," she ventured hesitantly, careful to omit who her father was. She made a face, hoping Ryan wouldn't want to know exactly what the *family business* in Philadelphia was.

He lifted a speculative brow. "But you have other plans?"

She nodded slowly. "We made a deal a year ago. He allowed me to take a year to make my business a success and make a profit. He respects successful people."

He raised one brow high. "And why are you here in Portland?"

"I want to land an exclusive deal with the largest chain of high-end bridal stores on the West Coast so I can fulfill the terms of our deal, which, by the way, expires in a week. This is my last chance."

Ryan nodded. "Okay, I get that. You're trying to snag a big account. If so, why are you backing out? I'd think the media exposure would be good for you."

This was getting dicey. She couldn't tell him about

the deliveryman recognizing her, and she couldn't tell him she wanted to succeed on her own, without the Sinclair name, because he didn't know she was a Sinclair. But she did owe him some kind of explanation. She settled on the truth—or part of it, at least. "The truth is that…well, I hate having my picture taken." She shrugged. "I'm painfully camera-shy."

He stared at her, then yanked his tie loose. "That's it? Is not wanting your picture taken really that big of a deal?"

She stood quickly, fire filling her chest. She fisted her hands on her hips and glowered at him, horrified at how much he sounded like her father, at how easy it was for him to flick aside her feelings. "Of course it's a big deal or I wouldn't be balking, would I?" She shook her head. "You just steamroll along, don't you?" she snapped, frustrated that things were spinning out of her control again. "Just like my father."

He froze, staring at her, then swung around and resumed pacing. "Sometimes I have to steamroll. I'd never be a success if I didn't go after what I want."

"Even if it hurts other people?" Oh, how she wished she wasn't so familiar with how someone else's needs always took precedence over hers. True, being camera-shy might seem like no big deal, but it was incredibly real to her.

He turned and looked at her with his intense blue eyes. "Is this going to hurt you?"

"Yes, it is." She knew from firsthand experience how much it hurt to surrender your hopes and dreams to somebody else. And she wished she could tell him that. But she couldn't tell him without revealing her real identity. Even so, she'd never be able to respect *herself* again if she didn't do everything in her power to succeed at what *she* wanted to do.

Now that she'd momentarily lost her sanity and signed the release, unless she could somehow stop the presses, her dream to succeed without her famous name might be in jeopardy, along with her dream to escape from Sinclair Banking.

Peter Sinclair came from a long line of arrogant, selfish men who had no qualms about making other people's lives hell to satisfy their own agenda.

Including Anna's mother.

She'd divorced Anna's father ten years ago because of his overbearing ways and lack of respect for her dreams of becoming a novelist. It wasn't until after she'd divorced him and sold her first book that he'd finally acknowledged her talents. After what she'd seen her mother go through, Anna knew that gaining his respect by succeeding on her own was the only way to make him see the value of what she wanted to do.

That might not happen now.

She sank down on the love seat and let her shoulders drop. How had she fallen into that oh-so-familiar trap and forgotten that Ryan had his own agenda, too?

How had she overlooked that he would use her to achieve his own goals, just like every other man in her life had?

She resisted the urge to bang her head against the wall, even though it might knock some sense into her.

How had she let her guard down so easily?

Ryan watched Anna's lush mouth curve downward into a frown and her slender shoulders slump as if she carried the weight of the world on them.

A major jolt of guilt zapped him. Obviously this whole thing was a bigger deal to her than he'd realized, or rather, than he'd wanted to realize.

Hell, her funky disguise should have been a clue as to how important her business was to her, the lengths she was willing to go to protect her dream.

A dream he could identify wholeheartedly with.

The look of utter defeat on her face troubled him. Even though she'd agreed to pose for the photo in the first place and had brought this on herself with her crazy scheme to prove things to her father, her obvious unhappiness set him on edge. She was a working girl out to make a success of her business in any way she could. He understood that, almost too much. She reminded him of himself seven years ago.

He moved toward her and hunkered down to her level. "I'm sorry this didn't turn out the way you wanted. But you did sign the release."

She bit her lip. "Yeah. I know. I shot myself in the foot. Good for you, though, right?"

He stood, really sorry she was so unhappy about all of this. "I guess so."

She wrung her hands, her mouth pressed into a little frown that hit him like a swift kick in his gut.

He took a seat next to her, wishing he could ignore how guilty he felt. Her delicate floral scent flowed over him and a slow fire kindled in his veins. He wanted to reach for her with everything in him, but didn't. Instead he quickly rose and stepped out of smelling range, needing to focus on the problem at hand, on anything but the womanly, sexy smell of her.

He shrugged out of his jacket and flung it on the couch. He hated feeling like he'd ruined her world, hated the sadness so obvious in her beautiful brown eyes. Even though it went against every bit of sense he possessed, he made a snap decision and said, "So let's go fix this."

She crossed her arms over her chest. "How?"

He yanked on his loosened tie, then jerked it from around his neck. "I can be very persuasive when I want to be." He threw his tie on the couch and started toward the door, then gestured for her to follow. "Let's go."

She picked up her bag and gave what distinctly sounded like a long-suffering sigh and walked by him. "I've got my car. I'll meet you there." She stopped at the door and turned, guilt showing in her brown eyes. "Thank you for this," she said. "I promise I'll help you come up with some other way to get the publicity you need for your foundation, okay?" She turned and walked out.

Although she had already stepped out of his office, the vague remnants of her soft, floral scent lingered in the air. He sniffed once, savoring the feminine smell, wondering if she always smelled so good.

He shoved his electronic planner into his pocket and started after her, shaking his head. He was being a fool. The way Anna smelled wasn't important.

As he followed her down the hall, appreciating the sway of her slim, jean-clad hips and the shape of her narrow back under her tight, white T-shirt, it didn't take much thought to figure out why he was so damn eager to help her out.

Her nerves a jangling mess, Anna met Ryan in the lobby of the large building that held the offices of the *Beacon*. He'd rolled up the sleeves of his white dress shirt, displaying his well-muscled forearms, and had unbuttoned the collar and top button, exposing a few golden chest hairs.

Looking away from those tantalizing curls, she made an effort to counteract the thoroughly crazy physical attraction she felt when he came within twenty feet of her.

She checked her watch: 7:00 p.m. "It's pretty late," she said, chewing her lower lip. "Maybe we should have called."

He shook his head and headed toward the hallway leading to the office. "No way. When you want something, it's always better to show up in person."

She followed him and just as they were about to open the door with the *Beacon* stenciled on it in black letters, it opened and a tall, attractive blond woman stepped through. Colleen.

Colleen stopped. "Hey! Anna." She smiled at Ryan. "Hello, Ryan."

Ryan nodded.

Anna cleared her throat. "Colleen, Ryan and I have a little…problem."

Colleen drew her brows together. "A problem?"

Ryan stepped forward. "Yeah," he said authoritatively. "About the picture. We're backing out of 'The Bridal Chronicles.'"

Anna had to admire his blunt attitude. And while her father was extremely blunt, too, Ryan was sacrificing his cause for *her,* something no man had ever done, especially her father.

"I'm sorry," Colleen said, her eyes wide. "But I can't—"

Ryan cut in. "Look, I know all about red tape and stuff like that, but Anna regrets her decision, and we both want to make sure our picture isn't included."

He gave Colleen a level stare. "It's important. I'm sure there's some way to make that happen."

Colleen held up her hands. "I'm sorry, guys. It's out of my hands. If you'd caught me a little earlier this afternoon, I might have been able to help, but as it is…" She trailed off, shaking her head.

Anna held her breath, a sick feeling moving through her like a bad case of the flu.

"What do you mean, 'as it is'?" Ryan pressed, his brows drawn low over his eyes. "What's going on?"

"Another article fell through, and 'The Bridal Chronicles' was moved ahead in the schedule." Colleen smiled apologetically. "Anna signed the release and the story went to press an hour ago. It's a done deal."

They were too late. The photo of her and Ryan was headed for the front page and there was nothing she could do about it.

Not a darn thing.

Anna closed her eyes, dreading the glaring spotlight poised to shine right at her. And Ryan. Together. For all the world to see. She was stuck well and good to Ryan as his pretend bride.

If that particular bit of torture wasn't bad enough, in no time her father would come storming into her life, his arrogance and antiquated familial expectations jammed on "full speed ahead."

A sinking feeling took root in her chest, and she was sure the unpleasant sensation wasn't going to go away for a long, long time.

And to make matters even more bleak, with her dad's arrival more than likely imminent, her life would only get worse.

*Sinclair Banking, here I come.*

## Chapter Four

Anna stood next to her car on the street around the corner from the *Beacon*. Cars drove by, speeding to make the stoplight at the intersection a half block down. A bus stopped to pick up passengers a few feet away, then closed its doors and accelerated, spewing exhaust, kicking up dust. She fanned herself against the late-afternoon heat, intensified by rush-hour traffic. What else could possibly go wrong today?

First that delivery guy had recognized her. Then she'd discovered "The Bridal Chronicles" had already gone to press, only to exit the building alone to find that she'd been given a parking ticket because she'd been in a hurry and had foolishly parked in a No Parking zone.

Muttering uncharacteristically dark thoughts under her breath, she heard heavy, crunching steps behind her. Her skin prickled.

*Ryan.*

"Are you all right?" he asked. He sounded concerned, and his deep voice sent ripples of pleasure down her spine.

She sat down on the curb. "I'm fine, I guess." She drew her eyebrows together and bit her lip. "Just mad." She held up the ticket.

He sank down on the curb next to her. "This city loves giving parking tickets. I've received three in the last month." He was quiet for a moment. "Did they nail you for the hefty fine?"

She eyed him, ignoring his question. "Aren't you afraid you'll get your designer suit dirty sitting on the curb like that?"

He shrugged. "Not really. Besides, I used to hang out on curbs all the time."

Surprise bounced through her. Ryan looked more like the golden-boy type who had never come near a curb in his life. The kind of guy she should avoid. "You're kidding," she said, turning toward him to see if he was joking. "You don't strike me as the type who'd ever hang out on a curb."

He looked off into the distance, his face shuttered, his eyes unreadable. "Is that so?"

Anna had the distinct impression he was dodging the subject. Lovely. She didn't want or need to know anything about him. Impersonal was just what she wanted, just how she needed things to be to remain immune to his masculine appeal.

They sat in silence for a time, which Anna didn't break. It was his turn to talk.

Finally he said, "I wish we could have stopped the photo."

She sincerely doubted it. "Oh, please. You're getting the publicity you want. You should be thrilled."

"I was willing to do without the publicity for your

sake," he pointed out. "I had no way to know the article would go to press this early."

"True. But it is convenient for you, isn't it?" she said, lifting a brow high.

He frowned, his eyes darkening to a deep, dark blue. "Dammit, Anna. Can't you be gracious enough to accept my apology?"

He was probably right. She'd never considered herself a particularly bitter person and she usually believed everything would work out for the best. She could only hope "The Bridal Chronicles" would produce some kind of positive outcome. Really, though, how could meeting Ryan and having her father descend on her possibly have a silver lining?

The tangle of dread inside of her told her that everything she'd worked so hard for was about to crash down around her.

She sighed and rested her elbows on her knees. "All right. I'll try to be gracious." Heaven knew that was what she'd been raised to do. In her world, a lady never raised her voice and was always polite and well mannered, no matter what the circumstance.

Sometimes she hated that.

"Good. I'm sorry about the photo. If I could have stopped it, I would have." He rose. "Now how about dinner?"

She snapped her head toward him, wondering at his abruptness. "Slow down. You're asking me out again?"

He grinned, the skin around his stunning blue eyes crinkling. "Sure. I'd like to make you feel better, and I'm starving." He rubbed his stomach. "How about we go down to the Rose Festival Fun Center on the waterfront and pig out on carnival food?"

His smile was infectious, even if his suggestion of pigging out was dangerous. One bite of a greasy hamburger and she'd never stop gorging.

Once again noticing his dimples, she gave him an answering smile, even though she was sure he was only asking her out to make himself feel less guilty. Besides, she might as well make the best of things. Perhaps if she went with him, she could press him for what she needed most—to make sure "The Bridal Chronicles" ended without any more photos or media exposure.

"You're always starving." As she took his offered hand and rose, holding on a bit longer than was necessary, she told herself she was only going with him to get what she needed. Agreeing to dinner had absolutely nothing at all to do with the sparks his touch caused, or with how much she loved his charming dimples and deep blue eyes.

If she told herself that enough, maybe she'd begin to believe it.

It was a wonderful night for a carnival.

The evening on the waterfront was balmy and remarkably dry for June, which she'd heard tended to be a cool, wet month in Portland. The smell of carnival foods filled the warm air—greasy French fries, sticky, sweet cotton candy, and cinnamon sprinkled elephant ears. The calls of the game hawkers—"three tries for a dollar!"—echoed across the tents, and the sound of a riverboat whistle, low and deep, floated on the warm breeze from the Willamette River. From the direction of the carnival rides, screams of either fright or joy reverberated in the warm evening.

As soon as they stepped through the gates, Ryan

looked at her, a sudden gleam in his blue eyes. "Let's hit the midway first, okay?" He pretended to throw a ball. "I'm feeling lucky tonight."

She smiled. "Fine by me," she replied, suddenly excited at the prospect of really experiencing the carnival, midway and all. Her father had always deemed carnivals and the like beneath them and had never, despite her begging, allowed her to go to one.

She was beginning to realize how many things she'd missed out on as a child, cocooned in the safe, boring little world her father had made for her.

They headed toward the ticket booth, and Ryan blithely bought a hundred tickets.

She looked at him, incredulous. "I thought you said you were feeling lucky."

"I am." He grinned like an excited little boy. "But when a Teddy bear's at stake, I want to be sure I have enough."

Anna fought to keep her jaw from sagging. She never would have guessed Ryan would care at all about something as sentimental as winning a Teddy bear at a carnival.

Since it was such a beautiful evening, the midway was jammed with people—young, old, couples and families. Ryan led her through the throng, looking left and right, stopping periodically to peruse certain stalls. Finally he pointed to his left. "Over there. The baseball toss."

Holding on to his big, warm hand—a mistake?—she followed him to a relatively uncrowded game stall at the very end of the midway.

They waited in line behind two gangly preteen boys who had fairly good arms but extremely bad aim. Both struck out several times without winning anything. As they were walking away, looking disappointed, Ryan held out some tickets. "Here, guys, why don't you try again."

Both boys looked as surprised as Anna was by Ryan's offer. "You sure, mister?" one of them said.

Ryan nodded. "I'm sure. Give it another try."

All smiles, the boys took the tickets and tried again.

One boy lucked out and knocked all of the milk bottles down with his three throws and won a small, stuffed snake. The other struck out again.

Ryan fed him tickets until the boy managed to finally knock down all three bottles to win a stuffed lizard. Grinning, the boys thanked Ryan profusely and ran off, their prizes clutched in their hands.

A warm spot growing inside of her, Anna looked at Ryan. "That was a very nice thing you did."

He shrugged as he handed his tickets to the hawker. "When I was their age and the carnival came to town, I could never managed to win anything. Just wanted to save them some well-remembered disappointment." The hawker handed him three baseballs, and Ryan faced the bottles, his face suddenly serious. After squinting at his target for a few seconds, he drew his arm back and hurled the ball at the stacked milk bottles.

All three crashed to the ground.

Ryan turned, his mouth pressed into a big smile. "Bull's-eye."

"I guess you've become a better shot," she said, her mind still on Ryan's reference to his youth. Curious about where he grew up, she was about to ask him about what town he meant, but the hawker turned back and his exclamation cut off her thought.

"Man, oh, man!" he shouted. "One shot and

they're down!'' He pointed to the stuffed animals hanging from a string suspended around the stall. ''Choose your prize.''

Ryan looked quizzically at her. ''You choose.''

She stared at him, surprised. ''Oh, no—''

''I insist. As a thank-you for coming with me tonight.''

Inclining her head in agreement, she nodded and looked up. Every animal under the sun hung from that string, but one immediately caught her eye. A small stuffed bear with fur the color of Ryan's hair. She pointed. ''That one.''

The hawker unhooked the cute little bear from the string with a hook and handed it to her. ''A bear for the lucky lady.''

She took the bear, feeling its soft, plush fur. ''He's adorable. I used to collect stuffed animals. My room was full of them.''

''Which was your favorite?'' Ryan asked, taking her hand again to lead her back into the crowd.

Trying to ignore the warmth traveling from his hand up her arms, she said, ''Probably a hippo named Retep.''

He looked down at her, his brow knitted. ''Retep?''

''I named all of my animals after people I care about.''

''Who in the world is Retep?''

She laughed. ''My father. It's Peter spelled backward.''

He raised an eyebrow.

''I know, I know, it's weird. What can I say? I was a strange little kid.''

''So what are you going to name that bear?'' He pointed to her bear.

*Nayr* immediately popped into her brain. It seemed appropriate to name the bear after the man who had won it for her. But she didn't really want to read too much into their "relationship," and naming the bear after Ryan seemed much too personal. "I don't know yet," she said. "I'll have to think about it."

Hand in hand, feeling more and more like they were a genuine couple on a date, Anna walked with Ryan up the midway toward the rides and food vendors, her unease growing bit by bit.

When they reached the giant Ferris wheel, Ryan led her into the line of people waiting to get on. "Let's ride."

She pulled back on his hand and looked up at the ride, towering at least fifty feet above them. "Uh, I don't know. I'm sort of…afraid of high places."

He wrapped a solid arm around her shoulder. "Oh, come on. It'll be fun. We'll get a bird's-eye-view of the whole carnival. You can hold on to me."

The thought of holding on to Ryan was almost as frightening—yet exciting—as thinking about riding the Ferris wheel. Trying to ignore how good his arm felt draped around her shoulders, she reluctantly let him take her back into the line. "I'm not sure about this, Ryan."

He looked at her, then pulled her closer and whispered in her ear. "If you're really afraid, then we won't ride. But I think you'll like it. The view is amazing."

Ryan's mouth so close to her ear and his big, muscular body pressed to her side sent hot chills radiating into her body. Oh, he felt so good and solid and warm and smelled so good….

The line moved forward and she let herself be

swept along, her crazy desire to stay close to Ryan overwhelming her fear of the ride. Ryan gave the man at the gate their tickets, and before long, they were seated side by side in the slightly swinging car.

The ride lurched to a start, and a rush of fear raced through Anna. With a squeak she closed her eyes and she instinctively pressed closer to Ryan.

He put his arm around her again and drew her to him. She pressed her face into his large shoulder and gripped his coat with one hand, her bear in the other.

"I guess there's something to be said for your fear," he huskily murmured into her ear again. "I like having you this close."

Her fear overrode the significance of what he was saying. Paralyzed, she willed the car to stop swaying. They moved higher and higher, stopping every time a car needed to be loaded, until they stopped at the very top of the wheel.

"Anna," he said gently. "Open your eyes and take a look."

She shook her head. "I'm afraid."

"I know." He squeezed her shoulder. "But sometimes we need to face our fears to conquer them. I promise you won't be sorry."

Maybe it was silly for her to be so frightened of this. Maybe she should at least *try* to face her fear. She could always close her eyes again if she was too nervous. Mustering her courage, she slowly opened her eyes, then lifted her head from his shoulder, her stomach dropping when the car swayed slightly at the motion.

She froze and let out another little squeak, squeezed her eyes closed again and grabbed for Ryan's hand.

"It's okay," Ryan said soothingly, stroking her hand. "The car is supposed to move a little. Open your eyes now so you can enjoy the view."

She nodded and opened her eyes bit by bit.

Ryan looked at her, smiling. "Brave girl. Look around."

Afraid to move, she just moved her eyes from one side to the other. "Very nice," she said, her mouth barely moving.

He chuckled. "You can move your head, you know. I promise, it'll be worth it. You can see clear across the river from here."

Nodding, she slowly turned her head to take in the view spread out before them.

And he was right. It was worth it.

The lights on the tents and the neon lights of the other rides, twirling and spinning below them, looked like bright, multicolored jewels glowing and moving in the dark. Further out she could see the Willamette River, flowing deep and wide as it moved through the middle of Portland, a giant ribbon of water. Several boats festooned with festive lights bobbed on the river in the darkness. The cars moving across the bridges spanning the river were visible, their headlights and taillights adding to the riot of colors before her.

She felt like they were on the top of the world.

The Ferris wheel started to move again, and a flash of fear moved through her. She gripped Ryan's hand but kept her eyes open, enjoying the panorama before her.

Ryan squeezed her shoulder and eased her close, resting his chin on her head. Acting on instinct, she snuggled down in next to him, feeling a strange sense of contentment move through her.

The Ferris wheel moved silently in the darkness, around and around. Relaxing, she let go of her fear and simply enjoyed the sights spread out in front of her and the feel of Ryan sitting beside her, his wonderful scent surrounding her, the warmth of his body seeping into hers.

And for a time, the rest of the world, and her fear, ceased to exist.

The Ferris wheel ride ended all too soon, although Anna acknowledged that it was probably for the best. She really shouldn't let herself enjoy Ryan's presence so much, especially not how wonderful his arms felt around her.

Past experience told her she could never let herself fall for him.

They stepped off the ride and made their way to the food area of the carnival. Anna had vowed to stay away from junky, fat-laden food, so she was delighted when she discovered a food stall selling grilled veggie pitas.

She ordered her pita, and Ryan ordered a huge double burger and fries from a starry-eyed teenage girl who couldn't stop ogling him. He met her shy stares with an appealing smile and silly joke. After he paid, she gave him an extra order of fries on the house.

He definitely knew how to turn on the charm.

Apprehension suddenly filled Anna. What if he decided to turn his considerable charm on *her* again? She didn't even want to think about it.

Anna followed him until they found a spot at a small table in the far corner of one of the huge dining tents. After they sat, her knees bumped Ryan's under the table and a crazy giddiness swamped her. She froze, wanting to leave her knees where they were, pressed up against his. But she couldn't let herself enjoy his touch or even let herself like him too much. Nothing could come of it except an aching heart and shattered dreams.

Being necessarily sensible, she slid back on her seat, her bear on her lap. But the tiny table/big Ryan combination made it impossible to escape his knees without falling off her chair. Desperate to keep his physical effect on her to a minimum, she tilted her legs at an uncomfortable side angle, trying to stay focused on her reasons for agreeing to come here with him.

*Forget the romantic Ferris wheel ride and Ryan's kindness to those boys. Make him promise to help end this whole chronicle disaster right away.*

Ryan dug into his food with gusto, obviously enjoying the greasy burger. Anna found her closeness to him had twisted her stomach into a lump and chased her appetite away.

"You like to eat, don't you?" she asked, smiling.

He inclined his head. "Yeah, I do. My...uh, my mom was a terrible cook, so I really appreciate good food."

She dubiously eyed the large basket of food in front of him. "That's good food?"

He held up a fry coated in ketchup. "Hey, this might not be gourmet eats, but it's filling and delicious."

Suddenly her veggie pita didn't look very appetizing.

Ryan chewed his burger, then threw her a questioning look. "Aren't you going to eat?"

She gave him a wan smile. "Uh, sure." She fiddled with the edge of her paper plate. "In a minute."

He wiped his mouth with a napkin. "You're still upset, aren't you?"

Now that he'd brought it up, she most certainly was. Even though she knew he was referring to her upcoming stint on the front page, which *was* bothering her, she was really more upset about how he always seemed to rattle her physically and emotionally, how he made her want to actually believe in true love. Even though she was wrapped up in the fantasy of weddings, true love wasn't something she could ever let herself believe in again.

She took a shaky breath and nodded. "I'm trying to look at the bright side and not worry about the picture, but my father…" She trailed off, belatedly realizing that she'd need to be careful talking about her father.

"Your father sounds like quite a guy."

She nibbled on a corner of her pita. "He's something else, all right. Men in his family aren't known for their gentleness, tact, nor understanding."

Ryan hesitated, a far off look in his eyes. "Yeah, I know how that is." He took a bite of his burger and chewed.

She waited for him to elaborate, but he didn't. "Was your father the same way?" she asked, her earlier curiosity about Ryan's family and youth coming back to her.

"Yeah," he bit out.

His reaction surprised her. "So you know what it's like to grow up with a father who expects too much?"

A muscle flexed in his jaw. "Let's keep the conversation on you, okay? My family's not up for discussion."

She sat back in her chair, a little stung. "Relax. I didn't mean to pry." Although she *was* interested in why he was so unwilling to talk about his family. What was he hiding?

He inclined his head. "All right. Go on about your father."

"Well, he's used to getting what he wants, and he's always had very specific ideas about what I should be doing. Now he wants me to join the family business instead of being a designer." She smiled wryly. "We've been butting heads my whole life."

"Have you tried talking to him about this?"

She shifted uneasily. "Some." Probably not enough due to her insane desire not to rock the boat. "But my father isn't easily swayed. I'm an only child, and he truly believes it's my duty to follow in his footsteps."

She sadly wondered if her father would ever understand how much she wanted to succeed at something of her own choosing, how much she wanted to carve her own path.

He wanted something from her that she couldn't give—the sacrifice of her dreams. She longed for the day when he would appreciate her choices, the day he would deem her worthy of his respect.

The day he would love her for who she was rather than what he wanted her to be.

"So why worry about what he thinks at all?" Ryan asked, breaking into her thoughts. "Just do what you want to do."

She snagged one of his fries and nibbled on it, savoring the greasy, salty taste. "I could, but he *is* my father, and despite his overbearing ways, I do love him. I'm hoping to show him that being a bridal designer isn't just some pipe dream, that's it's something I can succeed at.''

Ryan wiped his mouth with his napkin and pinned her in place with his darkening blue eyes. ''You're lucky he cares about you at all.'' He abruptly went back to his burger.

She stared at him, wanting to know what had put the unexpected shadows in his eyes, what had obliterated his earlier good mood. Even though he'd made it clear that his family wasn't something he wanted to talk about, she couldn't help but ask, ''You sound like you speak from experience. About caring, I mean.''

''Or not caring,'' he muttered around his bite of hamburger.

Her insides tightened. ''Did your parents not care about you?''

He finished chewing. ''Like I said, my family isn't up for discussion.'' He picked up a fry and pointed at her with it. ''Just be glad someone, somewhere cares about you.''

''Yes, well, my father might care about me, even though he shows it in an odd way, but I've met a lot of people who only care about themselves.''

''Oh, yeah? Like who?''

Oh, Giorgio, Randall, Jeffrey and Sam. She couldn't possibly tell him about how she'd made so many bad choices and blithely allowed so many men to reel her in with their good looks and charm.

She fidgeted and stared down at her food, suddenly sure she was making a huge mistake again. Here she was, sitting across from a man who had the power to blind her with his appeal and draw her in for the kill.

What was she doing, cozying up to another charismatic, gorgeous man?

"Hey." He took her hand. "What's wrong?"

His hand surrounded hers like warm steel. She looked at their entwined hands, his dark and large, hers pale and small.

A shiver of delight moved through her.

She liked the way her hand looked in his. And though she would always have her mom as a positive influence in her life, she still felt like there was a place inside of her where she'd been alone for a long, long time. A dark, hollow place that craved her father's approval and desperately wanted him to love her for who she was.

But that wasn't a space any man besides her father could ever fill. Seeing her hand in Ryan's reminded her of the truth.

He didn't care about her.

He was being nice to her and lending an ear and taking her on romantic carnival rides simply because he had an ulterior motive, just like every other man in her life.

Finally thinking clearly, she disengaged her hand from his and shot to her feet, clutching her bear in her hand. "I have to go."

And then she walked quickly from the tent, chiding herself. Because deep down inside she wished Ryan *did* care about her.

And that was as foolish a dream as wishing for her father's respect.

"Anna!" Ryan called, taken off guard by her unexpected departure. Vaguely worried, he rose and dashed after her, dodging tables. Why was she running away? One minute they were having a nice conversation, the next she was gone. She didn't seem like the type to run away from anybody unless something was really, really wrong.

Thankfully he was quicker than she was. He caught her behind the tent on the path that ran along the concrete wall next to the river. "Hey, wait!" He snagged her elbow.

She spun around, her eyes wide, her cheeks flushed. "Ryan, no. Let go."

"Only if you promise to stay put."

She considered him briefly, her eyes dark, gently pulling her arm from his grip. "I shouldn't."

He swiped a hand over his face. "Why not?"

"Look, can't you be mean or something and make this easier for both of us?"

He drew in his chin. *"What?"*

"Do something heartless."

"You want me to be heartless?" He screwed his face into a scowl. "Are you crazy?"

"Probably," she muttered, looking disgusted with herself. "I just want you to prove me right."

He shook his head slowly, totally confused. He took her elbow again, trying to ignore how soft her skin felt and how heat blossomed in him every time he touched her. "Right about what?" he asked, admiring her pretty brown eyes. "Tell me. Right now."

She searched his face briefly. "Let go and I'll tell you."

"Fair enough." He released her.

She stepped back, nibbled on her bottom lip, and pressed her stuffed bear to her chest. "Look, I'm sorry I…ran off. I just…well, the thing is…when you…''

"Spit it out—''

"You're pretending to be a nice guy, aren't you? You're pretending to have a heart.''

"Pretending?'' He slapped his forehead. "Dopey me. My blood just flows through my body all by itself.''

"Ha, ha,'' she said without humor. She looked off to the side and shifted from foot to foot.

He grunted. "It was supposed to be a joke and you look like a bee flew up your nose.'' He tried to look at her down-turned face without success. He straightened and let out a heavy breath. "Why do you think I'm putting on some act?''

She huffed. "Because…someone took advantage of me and I was too dumb to see it in time, all right?'' She pressed a hand to her mouth, looking like she was sorry she'd blurted that out.

Fire filled his chest, but he stifled his outrage to focus on the heart of the matter. Some guy had hurt her. To his surprise, her thinking that he was like some other jerk bothered him. Sure, he avoided serious romantic relationships to avoid the kind of slicing scorn Sonya had doled out to him. But he wasn't a liar and he wasn't pretending he was anything more or less than he was.

"Anna, I'm anything but heartless. And I don't think you're dumb.''

"I was the queen of dumb,'' she replied under her breath, then turned her clear brown eyes upward. "And how can I be sure you're not like…him?''

He held her gaze so she'd know he wasn't feeding her a line. "First of all, I'm always a man of my word. So when I say I'm not pretending, I'm not. And second, the key word in 'I was the queen of dumb' is 'was.' As in past tense. Over and done with. We all make mistakes—''

"You haven't. You've probably had the perfect life.''

He almost laughed out loud. She was so wrong, but he wasn't going to set the record straight. He'd worked his butt off to transform himself from the scraggly, hungry, neglected kid he'd been into the polished, successful man he was today. He'd had to fight like hell to rebound from what Sonya had thought of him—that he wasn't good enough. It would be difficult, maybe impossible, for him to admit to his squalid past.

Hell, he hadn't even been able to admit to the real reason that he liked to eat so much—because he'd grown up starving.

He turned away, wanting to hide any truth his expression might have held. "Yeah. Whatever.'' She viewed him exactly as he wanted everyone to see him—as a success from day one—and he wasn't about to ruin that image.

She would never see him in the same light if he did.

She was silent, so he turned to look at her, hoping she would drop the subject. What he saw was worse than any question she could ask him. Tears shimmered in her eyes, and that killed him. He stepped closer and put a hand on her shoulder. "Look, honey—''

She jerked away. "Don't call me honey.''

"Why not?'' he asked, trying to keep up with the twists and turns of her mind and their conversation.

"Because I like it too much!" She cut the air with both hands. "I like it when you're nice to me, and I like it when you call me honey, and I know it's all just an act."

He was flabbergasted, and strangely pleased, that he liked it when he called her "honey." "Hey, I already told you, it's not an act," he reiterated, surprised by how much he wanted her to believe him. He gently cupped her shoulders and stared right into her eyes again, willing her to trust him. "I swear it's not an act."

She stared at him like he'd grown an extra nose. "Don't you get it? Lies are easy to tell. I just can't be sure I can trust you." Her voice cracked and moisture pooled in her big, walnut-colored eyes.

And that almost broke his heart.

Acting on the instinct to soothe and protect her, he slid his arms from her shoulders around her back and pulled her close. She reared back, then crumpled against him, the bear still clutched in one hand.

Damn but he loved the feel of her small, slender body against his. "Hey, now, it can't be that bad," he murmured against her hair, inhaling the floral scent of her shampoo. Heat pooled in the lower half of his body and his heart expanded.

She snuffled against her shirt. "But it is. Men always want something from me."

"Well, thank you so much for grouping me in with all the other jerks," he said in a light voice, masking the hurt her statement caused.

She looked at him, clearly seeing behind his mask. "I'm sorry to put it that way, but I trusted a handsome, charming guy like you once, and he broke my heart."

The bastard. He understood her pain too well and wanted to pound the creep who'd hurt her into the pavement.

Out of necessity, Ryan ignored his primal instincts and focused on what she'd told him, which explained a lot. She was afraid to trust him because some creep had used her. He got that. Man, did he get that.

He tugged her back against him, crazily wishing he could turn back the clock and protect her from the sleazeball who'd done such a number on her. "Hon— Anna. I could never hurt you."

She lifted her head but didn't put any space between them. Her eyes shimmered in the approaching dark. "Then promise me this whole Bridal Chronicle thing is over. I know it would be good for your charity, and it bothers me that I have to ask you this. But I really, really don't want any more pictures printed."

He looked at her mouth as she spoke, wanting to close the distance between them and kiss her until his desire for her to trust him somehow magically seeped into her. But kissing her would be a mistake. After all the pain and bewilderment every "loving" relationship in his life had caused, he had to play it safe.

And he had to give her what she wanted.

Well, he didn't *have* to, but damn if he didn't want to. He wasn't about to add to Anna's troubles with any more media exposure. She reminded him so much of himself, trying to make something of herself, trying to prove that she could make it, despite the odds. He didn't want to jeopardize that, even if it would be good for the Mentor A Child Foundation. He could always find another way to raise awareness for them.

"All right," he told her, running his hands up and down her smooth, silky arms. "I can do that."

She smiled shakily at him, exposing straight, pearly teeth. "Thank you." She stood on her tiptoes, aiming her mouth for his cheek. He saw the chaste kiss coming and wanted to turn his head and catch her mouth with his and kiss her long, hard and deep. But he held back, taming his rebellious sanity. Her soft, full lips grazed his cheek and he bit back a groan.

She stepped back, her eyes wide. She pressed a hand he could have sworn was trembling to her mouth. "Sorry." She spun around, her head bent, and skittered over to lean against the concrete wall overlooking the river.

He stood frozen, trying to regain his control. He sure as hell liked Anna, and her soft kiss was the sexiest thing he'd come across in years. But he couldn't forget his cutting experiences with Sonya any more than Anna could forget the men who had hurt her.

He wanted to help her succeed. That was it.

He refused to let her affect him on any other level.

# Chapter Five

Anna sat cross-legged on a large pillow in her hotel room, meditating, newly christened Nayr the Teddy bear on her lap. For some reason, she'd given in to temptation and named him after Ryan.

Earlier, she'd called the hotel switchboard and asked them to hold all calls. She'd then put her favorite CD in her portable CD player, intending to get rid of the turmoil that had rocked her world since her brain had quit functioning and she'd lost herself into Ryan's arms at the Fun Center three days ago.

Even though she was supposed to be clearing her mind, she couldn't get rid of one thought:

*What in the world am I doing?*

How had she let herself get caught up in Ryan? She should have kept her distance at the Fun Center, but instead had plastered herself against his hard, broad chest—and had loved being there! And as if that wasn't bad enough, the feeling of his rough cheek against her mouth when she'd kissed his cheek still haunted her.

What would it be like to actually kiss him?

The mere thought sent heat billowing through her body.

Dear heaven, was she falling for another man like all of the other scheming, looked-good-on-the-outside but rotten-on-the-inside-men she'd foolishly trusted? Her stomach tightened. She could *not* make the same mistakes again. She wouldn't let herself.

She was stronger now, and had learned from her past mistakes. She was determined to succeed as a humble bridal designer, not as Anna Sinclair, so she needed to fall back on the things that always helped her get back on track.

Reassured, she resumed her meditation, soothed by the pounding tempo of the CD she'd chosen. After she meditated, she'd start reading that self-help book on "making the right choices" that she'd purchased.

After that, she had several designs that needed work—a velvet and fur fantasy gown she'd been designing for winter weddings, a simple, classic sleeveless silk sheath for summer, and a traditional lacy gown with a sweetheart neckline, bell-shaped skirt, and poofed sleeves that a Southern belle would wear. Thank goodness she had plenty of things to do instead of thinking about Ryan, and she had plenty of time to do it. She couldn't return to Philadelphia until Mr. Lewis, the president of Perfect Bridal, returned from attending to a family emergency on the east coast. This was the ideal opportunity to retreat, regroup and forget Ryan.

Thank the stars above one thing had gone her way in the last few days. Luckily the wind had blown her hair across her face in the photo that had been printed as part of "The Bridal Chronicles" in the *Beacon* two days ago and she wasn't easily recognizable. Thank heaven she also didn't look like the gawky, unattractive teenager who had landed on the cover of several Philadelphia publications when she'd been growing up.

Even so, she'd put up numerous prayers that she and Ryan wouldn't be chosen Best Wedding Couple, even though prayers were more than likely futile, even though Ryan had promised that "The Bridal Chronicles" would end here and now.

Though her face had been partially covered by her windblown hair, the picture of them had turned out beautifully. In the photo, Ryan was smiling adoringly at her, his dimples in plain view, and of course, he had looked better than any mortal man had a right to look, all tall, gorgeous male. She was smiling back at him like she loved him with all of her heart, like she was the happiest woman on earth. They were perfectly framed by a profusion of colorful rosebushes, which acted as a stunning foil for her flowing white, lacy dress and his dark tux.

They looked deeply in love.

But the picture was a sham, albeit a gorgeous sham. Being chosen Best Wedding Couple was probably inevitable, but it didn't hurt to hope the whole female population of Portland had suddenly gone blind. If not, she was counting on Ryan keeping his promise by making sure she didn't have to take part in any more photos.

In an effort to counteract her ominous thoughts, she concentrated on breathing deeply in tempo with the music. She would relax, think about positive things and find a way to avoid Ryan. Before long, he'd be nothing but a memory.

On a long breath, she chanted her mantra in time to the pounding bass of the music. "Giorgio is sleaze. Giorgio is sleaze. Giorgio is sleaze."

Somehow, that particular mantra always seemed to calm her down. Just as she'd managed to chase all thoughts and worries about Ryan from her frazzled mind, a pounding sounded on the door to her room.

She ignored the pounding. Maybe they would go away. "Giorgio is sleaze. Giorgio is sleaze. Giorgio is sleaze."

The pounding sounded again, louder now.

Sighing, she uncrossed her legs. So much for uninterrupted meditation. Standing, she grabbed Nayr, moved toward the door and opened it.

Her heart fell, then squeezed in her chest.

Ryan. In tight black jeans, scuffed leather boots, a black leather jacket, holding a motorcycle helmet. Looking like the bad boy, sexy male that he unfortunately was.

Stunned speechless, she glanced down at him, then jerked her gaze up to his face and froze, staring at his nose.

After a few seconds of weird silence, he made a face and waved. "Hello?" he yelled over the music.

She flushed. "Hold on." She went to her CD player and flicked the off switch, then moved back to the door.

"Metallica?" he asked, one brow raised. "I'm surprised the other hotel guests haven't complained."

"I always listen to heavy metal when I meditate. It relaxes me."

"Whatever floats your boat." He gave her an expectant look. "Can I come in?"

She didn't want him in her room, bending her common sense out of shape, breaking down her control like he had at the Fun Center. "I really don't think—"

"I've got some news."

"Let me guess," she said in a slow monotone. "We've been chosen Best Wedding Couple."

He nodded, looking sincerely sorry. "Yeah."

Her stomach twisted into a tight knot. She fell back a step, then swung around and paced the small entrance to her room, one hand clenched, one hand gripping Nayr. "I knew it," she muttered darkly. "I just knew it." Now her plan to avoid Ryan was history and she'd end up on the front page of some sleazy tabloid. Not only would she look terrible, her true identity would be up for grabs.

"Can I come in?" Ryan asked again from the doorway.

She sighed heavily, going over all of the reasons in her mind why she shouldn't let him in.

She was attracted to him.

He was the kind of man she had to stay away from.

The list went on and on.

"Look," he said, cutting her off, glancing at his watch. "I'm meeting a friend for the second part of my ride in half an hour. Can I come in or not?"

She wanted to say no. She really did. But being the considerate person she was, she couldn't turn him away, especially since he'd made a special trip here to talk to her.

Swallowing her trepidation at having big, incredible, biker Ryan in her tiny hotel room, she nodded.

"All right, you can come in. But just for a little while."

"Thanks." He stepped inside, and gestured to the overflowing hotel garbage can she'd set next to the door. "Excess garbage?"

"My designs always suffer when I'm upset." She propped Nayr against the pillows on one of the beds. "I'll be lucky to ever design another decent dress again."

His eyes held on her. "You're still upset about the photo I take it."

"What else would I be upset about?" She turned from his intense blue eyes and moved further into the room, unable to ignore the shiver of pleasure his look caused. Obviously the photo was only half of the problem. Her thoroughly unacceptable attraction to him was the other half.

He followed her in, putting his helmet on the bed closest to the door. "Yeah, I figured you'd be upset. That's why I came here to deliver the news in person."

His caring about her feelings surprised and touched her. "You came here just to tell me this? Why didn't you just call?"

He lifted one broad, leather-encased shoulder. "I was out anyway. Do you mind if I sit?" he asked, gesturing to the bed nearest him.

"Go ahead."

He lowered himself to the bed, wincing.

Concern rolled through her. "What's wrong?"

"I participated in a charity event yesterday, and the three-legged race was a killer."

She suppressed the urge to laugh. "You hurt yourself in the three-legged race?"

"Hey, you should have seen the kid I was hooked to. He was so small he wasn't much help. I wasn't allowed to pick him up, so I ended up sort of dragging him along and I wrenched my leg in the process. He's fine, though." He leaned back and propped one leg on the opposite knee. He rubbed his calf, grimacing.

The sight of him rubbing his leg sent heat rushing through her. Oh, how she wanted to kneel down next to him and rub that calf herself…

She swallowed heavily. "So why did you?" she asked, her voice high and tight. "Come here. To see me. I mean, if you're so sore." Darn it all, she couldn't even manage to string a coherent sentence together.

"I felt bad when I found out about Best Couple, and as I said, I wanted to tell you myself, especially after I promised no more wedding stuff."

Anna wasn't used to a man really caring about her feelings. Uneasy, she sat on the edge of the desk chair and took a deep breath, determined not to let his presence rattle her. "I doubt you feel *that* badly. Your pet charity is going to get all kinds of exposure out of this, just as you wanted." Which, really, was a good thing. She felt like a heel for even worrying about any of this at all.

"Look, whether you believe me or not, I do feel bad that things didn't turn out the way you wanted."

"But this will be really good for the Mentor A Child charity. Which is great. At least one good thing will come out of this."

"I hope so," he said. "Anything that gets the organization in the public eye is good."

She stood and walked over to stare out the window at the sight of the sun glinting off the buildings of downtown Portland. "Yes, well, the public eye isn't that great for me." She took a deep breath and let it out. "Thank goodness my face was partially hidden in the photo."

He moved behind her. "You still looked beautiful," he said into her ear in a low, deep voice. His warm breath feathered her neck as he leaned in so she could smell his spicy scent and feel the warmth of him so close to her.

Even though she doubted his words, her heartbeat accelerated. Trying to ignore the way her body always enthusiastically responded to him, she swallowed and said, "Thank you."

He put his hands on her shoulders. She softly gasped. Warmth rippled down her arms and flowed into her body, and she had to fight to keep herself from pressing back into him, from turning her head around and searching for his kiss.

"You were the perfect bride."

She gave an uneasy little laugh and turned to look up at him. "Hey, I know the dress designer."

He was so close her breath left her in a rush. The light from the window illuminated his eyes, framed by his dark lashes, making them look like the brilliant blue sky on a summer day. The urge to lose herself in his touch and kiss almost overwhelmed her flagging common sense.

He kept his intense blue eyes on her, but dropped his hands from her shoulders and stepped back. "It had nothing to do with the dress, Anna, even though the dress was very pretty. Your true beauty comes from the kind of person you are—a strong, hardworking, down-to-earth woman struggling to make it on her own. Some day you'll make some lucky guy a wonderful *real* bride.''

"I doubt it," she said, guilt for lying to him shooting through her. He had no idea how un-down-to-earth she really was as the heiress to one of the largest banking dynasties in the country. And even though his thinking of her as marriage material warmed a place deep inside of her, the loss of his touch made her feel suddenly empty and alone.

"Don't you believe in true love, happily ever after and stuff like that?" He looked intently at her. "Most women do."

She smiled wryly and inclined her head. "I used to be an incurable romantic. But I'm not anymore." She moved to the table and took a sip from her water glass. "To love I'd have to trust, and…well, to tell you the truth, I highly doubt I'll be able to do that again."

"My sentiments exactly." He paused. "About love, I mean."

She widened her eyes, surprised. Ryan was more like her than she'd realized. "You don't think that stuff exists?"

He shook his head. "No way. My parents didn't have time to love me. They only had time to fight. And…I guess you could say I've been burned, which pretty much cured me of ever believing in anything, really."

"You're kidding. What woman would do that?" she asked before she could stop herself.

"Trust me. They're out there." His eyes darkened and he turned away.

Obviously he'd been wounded like she had. Oh, how she wished that she was the kind of woman who could heal him. But she wasn't. Her negative track record with men had seen to that. "I'm sorry," was all she could say.

He rolled a broad shoulder. "I learned an important lesson, one I should have learned from my parents. Love is a damn myth. It doesn't exist."

Somehow, it saddened her to know that this incredible man didn't want to love. "I'm surprised that we agree about this. You're such a generous guy."

"I can be generous without loving, you know. Love is nonexistent, period."

They did have that in common, and when she really thought about it, she didn't want to share anything with him, especiàlly not something as personal as feelings about love. She paced by Ryan, biting her lip.

He rubbed his neck. "Look, I know you didn't want any of this media attention, but I want it for the foundation. I don't want to be selfish, but I can't set aside my own priorities, either. For the record, I'm really torn about what's happened. I want to protect you, but I want the publicity for my charity."

Either he was a very good actor or he was truly sincere. She always liked to think the best of people and wanted to believe the latter, but that had led to trouble in the past. "I doubt you're that torn. Maybe, if I'm lucky, being chosen Best Couple will be the end of it."

He shot her an apologetic glance. "No such luck."

She fisted her hands at her sides, preparing for bad news. "What do you mean?"

"As Best Wedding Couple, we're expected to go to the Portland Bridal Show and participate in a mock wedding. On live TV. Tomorrow."

Sharp blades of panic chopped through her. "But you promised—"

"I know, I know," he said, cutting her off. "I've already been to the *Beacon* to try to get us out of it—"

"How hard did you try?"

"I gave it my best shot."

Okay. He probably had. But that didn't change the fact that exactly what she feared would happen was happening.

A media blitz that could reveal her real identity and might plaster her picture all over the country.

Like it or not, she was on a crash course for a publicity whirlwind and lots of cameras. Worse yet, Ryan, one of the most attractive men she'd ever met, was along for the ride.

Mock wedding, media circus, handsome Ryan.

Three things that scared her to death, three things she had to find a way to deal with. Right now. Before she got in any deeper than she already was.

And before her foolish heart repeated the past and caved to temptation.

An ominous silence scraped across Ryan's nerves.

"I can't do it," Anna stated a few moments later, her clear amber eyes hard.

Ryan's admiration for her grew. And that irritated him. He'd come here to break the news about the mock wedding in person, partly to soften the blow, partly to help take the edge off his own guilt.

But he hadn't come here to admire her, or even because he liked her, even though she was proving to be very fascinating, not to mention incredibly attractive. In her beige chinos and plain white T-shirt, her hair in a no-nonsense ponytail and not a bit of makeup on her face, she had no right to look so damn beautiful. His attraction to her merely complicated an already muddled situation, and he hated complications.

He had to get this whole situation back on track. His track. "You can't just back out."

She straightened an already neat stack of sketches on the desk. "You promised to help me, and I expect you to live up to that promise. Pay up, buddy."

He *had* promised, and he'd tried to back out for Anna's sake. But the guy in charge at the newspaper had made it clear that backing out wasn't option at this late date. When Ryan had been given the go-ahead to set up a fund-raising and informational booth for the Mentor A Child Foundation at the wedding show, he'd had to agree. All he had to do was convince Anna to cooperate—again.

He scoured his mind for a way to turn her around. He looked around the room, noting, with pleasure, that she'd propped the bear he'd won at the carnival on the bed. He then looked at her design sketches on the desk, featuring a flowing, lacy gown with a high neck and tight sleeves. Maybe a simple reminder of how good this wedding show would be for *her* business would be enough. He was betting—and hoping—that her desire to succeed as a designer would override her desire to avoid the media and that the good person inside of her would relent for the sake of his charity.

He gazed at her speculatively. "I've been given permission to set up a booth at the show for the foundation, so, yes, I want this pretend wedding gig. But this would be fantastic exposure for you, too. Have you thought of that?"

She froze, her hands on a sketch. She slowly looked up at him. "Of course I've thought of that. That's what got me into this whole mess in the first place."

He tilted his head to the side. "Okay, so let's look at this from a different angle. Have you landed the account you're after yet?"

Anna straightened. A scowl marred her forehead. "No."

"Why not?"

"The man in charge hasn't made a decision yet."

"Have you met with him, presented your designs?"

"Yes."

"And what did he say?"

"He liked my designs, but..." She trailed off and looked away.

"But what?" he pressed, needing something to work with.

"Well, he was uneasy about giving the account to such an inexperienced, unheard-of designer."

He snapped his finger. "Bingo. You won't be nearly so unheard-of if your dress is featured on TV, will you?"

She scowled at him. "You're not playing fair."

He spread one hand, palm up. "Hey. I want the bridal show to help with my charity, a good cause I'm pretty certain you'd feel good about helping. Your business would benefit, too. I'd say that's very fair. Come on, Double-O-Seven. You know this is the right thing to do."

She crossed her arms over her chest, glaring tawny fire. She turned and paced around the hotel room, muttering under her breath and wringing her hands.

After about five trips in a circle, she turned back to him. She huffed. "All right, you win. And you're right. I will feel good that your charity will benefit. I've been feeling really guilty about that all along." She moved to the desk and straightened the sketches again. "You knew exactly how to manipulate things around to get the publicity for your foundation, didn't you? You're very good at that."

He cringed inwardly at the implication that he was manipulating her, surprised that what she thought about him mattered to him at all. "You want your business to succeed," he said as offhandedly as he could manage. "That's your need, not mine."

After a long pause she said, "I'm glad you realize that because I want to make it clear that I'm doing this for me, not to help you out, even though I'm pleased that your charity will benefit."

He slowly nodded. "Fine."

However, when Anna turned her back on him and rummaged through her briefcase, shutting him out, her words troubled him.

She wasn't doing this to help him out.

An odd, unexpected emptiness grew inside of him until he felt dull and hollow.

More solitary than ever.

And for the first time since Sonya had shoved his heart through a meat grinder, he wondered whether what he'd focused on for the last few years—his business, which was his dream and salvation—was going to be enough after all.

# *Chapter Six*

Anna looked down at the luxurious, creamy material surrounding her and sighed. She couldn't believe she was decked out in another of her wedding dresses.

But here she stood in a tiny, drab dressing room at the Portland Exhibition Center, swathed in acres of heavy satin, trying to stand still while the show coordinator hooked the tiny pearl buttons that marched up the back of the dress Anna had designed.

The Portland Bridal Show was in full swing, and she and Ryan were expected to make their grand entrance in ten minutes—as bride and groom.

She fidgeted, her hands clenched at her sides.

*Pretend,* of course, but even a fake wedding ceremony with Ryan was enough to turn the butterflies that had taken up residence in her stomach into giant birds with sharp claws and beaks.

Nothing new at all. She'd been a basket case since yesterday when Ryan had so eagerly pointed out that being part of this fake wedding ceremony would be good for her business, too, not to mention that his charity would be getting what it needed.

So, she was taking his advice and trying to be practical and focus on the positive. She'd put on a brave face and would make it through this whole thing with Ryan at her side if it would help land the Perfect Bridal account.

If it would help her prove herself.

"Please try to hold still," the woman said, tugging on the back of Anna's dress. "These buttons take a long time to hook."

Anna made a conscious effort to hold still when all she wanted to do was squirm. "Are you almost done?"

Another tug. "Almost."

To Anna's utter irritation, Ryan had burrowed into her consciousness like a pesky termite. She'd been unable to forget his sparkling blue eyes, easily given smile, and the glimpses of a tender, understanding man that tempted her to forget the brutal lessons about love she'd learned the hard way.

Ryan made her want to get to know him better—lots better. The image of him in a three-legged race with a little kid had been particularly hard to ignore.

For the hundredth time she chastised herself, remembering why Ryan *seemed* as if he cared about her. It was an act crafted to get her to do what he wanted. Nothing more. She couldn't forget that, couldn't make another bad choice that would hurt.

"There you go," the woman said, smoothing the back of Anna's dress, which, thank goodness, lacked a train. "You can turn around now."

Anna turned and faced the mirror on the wall. She

gasped, even though she'd designed the dress and knew exactly what it looked like—on the hanger.

The simple empire waist gown, the color of a lustrous pearl, made her look like a fairy-tale princess. The tight-fitting, scooped bodice had tiny pearls sewn over every inch, and the long, lacy sleeves hugged her shoulders and arms like a second skin. The dress fell from beneath her breasts in a shimmering wave of fabric to skim the floor. A hairstylist had pulled her hair into a high, tight bun surrounded by a pearl-encrusted tiara with a short tulle half-veil, a necessary, disguising accessory that she had feared would be tacky but looked absolutely stunning with the dress.

She looked like an honest-to-goodness bride.

But she wasn't. It was long past time for her to put away her girlish fantasies about love and marriage and face the fact it wasn't meant for her.

She designed wedding dresses for other women. Not herself.

Without warning, a wave of sadness pervaded her. Surprised by the emotion, she abruptly turned away from the make-believe bride in the mirror and shook the sadness off. She had no time for regrets.

She clenched her jaw. "Let's get this over with."

The young redhead nodded and followed her out of the dressing room door into the hallway that led backstage.

As Anna walked down the long, echoing passage, she repeated her instructions to herself.

Spend as little time as possible with Ryan.

Pay no attention to Ryan's stunning smile and gorgeous eyes and seemingly generous personality.

Get the ceremony over with.

Try not to worry about the cameras…

Her stomach clenched, but by the time she reached the end of the hallway, she thought she had herself under control.

Until she opened the door to the back part of the stage and stepped through into the brightly lit area.

Ryan stood in the wings, looking like an absolute dream in a black tuxedo, his gilded hair shining like a burnished penny under the bright stage lights. He was surrounded by a bevy of smiling, awestruck women.

Anna stopped in her tracks, barely able to breathe, her eyes wide. An unfamiliar feeling crawled through her stomach like a fat lizard, overriding the sudden, strange ache in her chest.

*Why, I'm jealous!*

She stood like a statue, watching him joke and tease and laugh with those adoring women and she wanted to rush over and scratch all of their eyes out.

She wanted him to smile and laugh like that with *her.* She wanted to be the center of his universe, darn it.

She fell back a step and pressed a quivering hand to her waist. She wished she could sweep aside the disgusting truth, tell herself that she wasn't a shallow, almost lovesick fool. But she couldn't. She was out and out, green-to-the-gills jealous of every single woman there.

Her hopes to remain unaffected by Ryan sank like bricks in water. Keeping herself cool around him had lasted exactly a nanosecond.

Chewing her lip, she glanced around, at once noticing a tall, dark-haired young woman hovering in the wings across the stage, chewing the end of a pencil, a small notepad in her hand. The woman was doing her best to appear casual, but it was obvious to Anna that the woman was watching her.

Another reporter?

*Wonderful.* The icing on the cake. It was becoming glaringly evident that even though Ryan's foundation would benefit, this whole wedding/Ryan experience was going to be much worse than Anna had thought.

And she'd thought it was going to be pretty darn bad.

Ryan tuned out some dumb joke a tall brunette was droning on about and looked around, wondering where Anna was.

He spotted her by the stage door. His breath stalled in his lungs and he could have sworn a two-by-four had materialized out of thin air and whacked him in the gut. He had to remind himself not to drop his jaw.

She was a vision he wouldn't forget as long as he had a heartbeat. The cream-colored wedding dress she wore fit her to perfection, emphasizing her slender upper body and full breasts. The shimmering material fell like silk around her, wrapping her in a lustrous haze that made her skin glow as softly as a freshly picked pearl. Her dark red, shiny hair had been pulled tightly onto the top of her head with a shimmering crown holding a short veil. While the style was severe, the whole thing emphasized her exquisite bone structure and her creamy, smooth complexion.

When he managed to take in a breath, he noticed the odd expression she wore. He frowned, trying to decipher the look, knowing instinctively that her strange little pout went much deeper than the look of dread he'd pretty much expected. He came up empty,

# The Silhouette Reader Service™ — Here's how it works:

If offer card is missing write to: The Silhouette Reader Service, 3010 Walden Ave., P.O. Box 1867, Buffalo, NY 14240-1867

NO POSTAGE
NECESSARY
IF MAILED
IN THE
UNITED STATES

## BUSINESS REPLY MAIL
FIRST-CLASS MAIL    PERMIT NO. 717-003    BUFFALO, NY

POSTAGE WILL BE PAID BY ADDRESSEE

SILHOUETTE READER SERVICE
3010 WALDEN AVE
PO BOX 1867
BUFFALO NY 14240-9952

*Play the*

# Lucky Hearts *Game*

and get...

## 2 FREE BOOKS
## and a FREE MYSTERY GIFT...
### YOURS to KEEP!

*yes!* I have scratched off the silver card. Please send me my *2 FREE BOOKS* and *FREE mystery GIFT*. I understand that I am under no obligation to purchase any books as explained on the back of this card.

*Scratch Here!*

then look below to see what your cards get you... 2 Free Books & a Free Mystery Gift!

## 315 SDL DU6R                    215 SDL DU67

FIRST NAME

LAST NAME

ADDRESS

APT.#

CITY

STATE/PROV.

ZIP/POSTAL CODE

(S-R-09/03)

Twenty-one gets you
**2 FREE BOOKS**
and a *FREE MYSTERY GIFT!*

Twenty gets you
**2 FREE BOOKS!**

Nineteen gets you
**1 FREE BOOK!**

**TRY AGAIN!**

Offer limited to one per household and not valid to current Silhouette Romance® subscribers. All orders subject to approval.

though, and chalked up her weird scowl to simple irritation at having to take part in this fake ceremony.

He excused himself from the cluster of women around him and made his way toward Anna. Her expression didn't improve as he drew near. He could almost imagine a tiny rain cloud hovering above her head, cartoon style.

He smiled, hoping a grin would be infectious, but she just pressed her lips together in a tight line. Cute little frown lines formed between her eyes and he had the absurd urge to reach out and smooth those creases away. Or maybe kiss them away...

*Back on track, Cavanaugh.* He needed to keep his hands, and his kisses, to himself. Touching or kissing her would border on disaster. If he did, then he'd want her, and he didn't want to want her.

"Hey, Anna." He raised a hand in greeting.

She smiled, but the quick pull of her mouth upward looked tight and forced. She inclined her head sharply in the direction of the group of women he'd just left. "That's quite the little entourage you have there. You attract all kinds of attention, don't you?" She sounded almost huffy.

He frowned. "What?"

She crossed her arms tightly against herself. "All of those women. Are they your fan club?"

He pulled in his chin. She might hate having to be part of this show, but from what he'd seen of her in the few weeks since they'd met, she didn't seem like a bitter or mean person.

In fact, she seemed like a really nice gal, one he liked a lot. Maybe too much.

He looked at her intently. "What's stuck in your craw?"

She stared at him for a long second, her lips tight and quivering. She blew out a fat breath, and then her face softened. "Forgive me," she said softly. "I just wasn't expecting...uh, well that is, I was surprised to see you...with all of those women."

Understanding hit him like a whack upside of his head. He leaned in and said in a low voice, "Woo-hoo! You're jealous, aren't you?"

She drew back, her nostrils practically quivering in stricken indignation. "I am most certainly not jealous. That's totally ridiculous. Why would I be jealous? I'm just...surprised, that's all."

"Methinks thee doth protest too much," he quipped, even though he was serious. Pleasure un-furled inside of him at the thought of Anna possibly liking him.

But he crammed the good feeling back into its cage and shoved it where he couldn't feel it. He didn't want to care about how she felt about him, and damn it, he wouldn't care. Sonya had taught him the im-portance of that.

Anna remained silent, her bottom lip clamped be-tween her teeth, her expression hovering between stony silence and outright misery.

Call him crazy, but seeing her so upset blew his vow not to care about her to pieces. "Hey, now," he said softly. "What's wrong?"

"I'm not jealous."

For her sake, he wasn't going to argue. "Okay. I believe you. Just don't get all upset about nothing, all right?"

"I'm not upset. I'm just...well, I don't want to do this. You know I hate cameras."

He still felt bad about her having to take part in

this silly wedding on TV. But it was too late to back out now. They were locked into doing this show, and if anything could drum up awareness for Mentor A Child, it was this hokey bride show and the booth he'd had set up in the exhibit hall.

Trying to ease her anxiety, he said, "Look, it'll all be over soon and then you can forget everything about 'The Bridal Chronicles.'"

"I hope so, because all of this," she said, indicating the large stage, "scares me to death."

Before he could reply, a man yelled, "Thirty seconds, everyone!"

Ryan straightened his silk cravat-style tie and held out his arm to Anna. "Are you ready to marry me?"

She froze, looked at his arm and then up at him. "We really have to do this, don't we?"

The panic he saw in her eyes was like a swift jab in the belly. Yes, he wanted the public exposure, not only for Mentor A Child, but for his image, too. He reminded himself that he couldn't help kids if the foundation's Board of Directors believed Joanna's lies about him being a slave driving, overdemanding, arrogant employer and decided his perceived public persona wasn't good for their cause.

But Anna's panicky look really got to him, really cut him. He didn't like making her unhappy, didn't like knowing he'd put a shadow in her eyes. "Not if you don't want to," he surprised himself by saying.

Her eyes widened at his response. Obviously she was shocked that he was willing to cut her a break. She bit her bottom lip, and he could imagine the heated debate going on in her head. He'd given her an out. Was she going to take it?

After an excruciating pause, she sucked in a deep

breath and placed her hand under his outstretched arm and rested it lightly between his shoulder and elbow from below. The moment her hand touched him, heat traveled through his arm to his chest.

"No," she said. "Even though I hate being in front of cameras, this *will* be good for my business, and your foundation, too. Let's get this over with." With her free hand she flipped her veil down over the upper half of her face.

Relief spread through him. She looked up at him again and her clear, dark topaz eyes met his. He stood spellbound, lost in her gorgeous gaze, totally unaware of anything but the woman holding on to him, preparing for their pretend wedding.

And damn if he didn't have the craziest wish that this ceremony was the real thing.

"Come on, bride and groom," a voice called, interrupting his strange little fantasy. "It's time to get married."

Ryan jerked his eyes away, trying to get a hold on himself. As he woodenly walked toward the curtain on the stage, he wondered what in the world was wrong with him. This wedding wasn't anywhere near real, and he should be glad. Anna might be the ideal pretend bride, but that's all she was. A fake bride to help the foundation.

But that didn't explain at all why he'd been so pleased she was jealous. Or why he fantasized that this was more than just a play, acted out for the bridal show. Or why the prospect of a honeymoon with her filled him with a raging heat he couldn't seem to get rid of. The very thought of her in a lacy, revealing nightgown, lying on a bed with her hair spread out around her, her arms outstretched to him…

His body responded in a natural way, which was a bad thing considering they were seconds from getting "married" in front of hundreds of people. Taking a deep breath, he forced all those disturbing thoughts from his head, determined, out of long enforced habit, not to dwell on what he couldn't explain.

Because for the life of him, he couldn't make sense of his crazy attraction to Anna after being burned so badly before.

The curtains opened with a *whoosh* and the bright overhead lights nearly blinded Anna. The large exhibit hall spread out before them, bisected by a long, narrow runway surrounded by people.

An audible hush fell over the crowd and hundreds of eyes fastened on her. Her cheeks warmed and a rush of bitter, cloying anxiety poured through her, and she prayed she didn't trip over her own feet and make a total fool of herself in front of the world. She tightened her grip on Ryan's thick, solid upper arm, taking comfort in his strength. He patted her hand, and she relaxed a tiny bit.

Until she noticed the television cameras aimed at her, symbolically beaming her picture directly to the whole world.

The media was everywhere.

A sudden rush of fear filled her and she wanted to run away and hide.

Ryan placed his big, warm hand over hers and leaned close to her ear. "Hey, it's okay," he whispered. He probably looked like an adoring groom murmuring sweet nothings in his beloved bride's ear.

That was as far from the truth as it could get.

Even though she wasn't his beloved bride, his

words and touch calmed her in a way she didn't understand. Maybe it was because she wasn't in this alone. Or maybe it was his soothing voice and reassuring touch. Whatever it was, she managed to take a deep breath and corral her overwhelming need to bolt.

Instead she plastered a smile on her face, reminded herself that this might help her land the Perfect Bridal account and ensure her future as a wedding dress designer. Taking a deep, shaky breath, she forced herself to walk next to Ryan down the runway.

An announcer gave their names and described her gown and Ryan's tux. After what seemed like an hour, but was really only minutes, they were back on stage, standing in front of a short, old man with gray hair and glasses dressed in a minister costume.

He smiled benignly. "Dearly beloved, we are gathered here together…"

Anna stood stock-still as he recited the short ceremony, sounding remarkably official. Halfway through, Ryan laid his hand over hers and gently squeezed, which, again, was surprisingly comforting. She curled her fingers around his and held on for dear life.

"You may now kiss the bride," the minister announced.

A hush fell over the crowd.

*Kiss?* No one had mentioned anything about a kiss! She looked up to Ryan who, oh Lordy, Lord, had turned toward her and reached for her with his free hand, his mouth pulled into a lazy, sexy, come-here-and-kiss-me grin.

Her knees trembled and she almost fainted into a heap of cream satin on the floor.

Apparently he had no problem with kissing her in front of hundreds of people. She could only stand, frozen in total shock, as Ryan put his big, hot hands on her shoulders and tugged her close.

Time slowed to a crawl. One of his hands came up and gently tilted her chin upward. With every long second that passed she was sure he would regain his sanity and stop this madness. But as he bent his head, she realized he had no intention of stopping anything.

He was crazy. He was definitely going to kiss her. For real. On live TV.

Worse yet, she wanted his kiss more than anything she'd ever wanted in her life.

# Chapter Seven

Her heart pounding like a jackhammer, Anna let Ryan settle her against his big, hard body. His spicy scent surrounded her, making her light-headed. His hand slid from her chin across her jaw and behind her head to hold her steady. Instinctively she slid her arms around his waist and pressed them against his hard, muscled back. He dropped his head and she closed her eyes and waited, her heart ready to spring from her chest and dance around on the ground by itself.

A long, agonizing second later, his mouth gently brushed hers, once, twice and then he pressed down and settled his lips over hers.

*Oh, yes!* His lips were firm but soft and so, so warm. His minty breath washed over her and she sighed in delight, opening her mouth slightly.

He groaned under his breath and slanted his mouth on hers, deepening the kiss, touching her lower lip with his tongue. Shocked by the deep, searing pleasure overtaking her, she tentatively darted her tongue out, wanting to experience every facet of his wonderful kiss.

His tongue touched hers and she thought she would combust on the spot. Pleasure and a profound, yet strange sense of rightness mixed inside of her, making it impossible to think about anything but wanting him closer, and then closer still.

She fisted her hands around his tux jacket. On a whimper she opened her mouth and pressed nearer, hazily thinking in the back of her stupefied brain that she had suddenly found something rare and wonderful.

Loud applause jerked her back to reality. She dazedly yanked back from Ryan, breathing like she'd run a marathon, and looked up at him. He was breathing heavily, too. Good heavens, he looked like their kiss had been as exciting and as earth-shattering to him as it had been to her!

Not very likely. Mr. Cool affected by a mere kiss?

She took a shaky step away, shocked by how easily she'd lost control. This was a *show,* for pity sake, not real.

What did the fact that this was just a show have to do with it? Would her response to his kiss be less shocking if the kiss had been real? A mind-exploding kiss was a mind-exploding kiss no matter how she looked at it. At least she could rest assured she wouldn't be kissing him again.

That was a good thing, right?

As she scrambled around in her suddenly uncooperative mind, trying to scrounge up an acceptable answer to her mental question, the minister said something. Ryan took her hand and tugged her back down the runway. The crowd clapped and Anna walked along next to Ryan in a cloudy haze.

Ryan led her back onstage. She followed him on shaky legs as he made his way backstage. People involved in the show congratulated them and thanked them as they passed by. Thankfully, the reporter she'd noticed earlier wasn't around.

He jerked open the first door he encountered and led her through. Luckily it was an unoccupied dressing room.

He slammed the door behind them, and before she could utter a word, he took her shoulders and gently pushed her against the wall. Surprised, Anna looked up at him, her stomach fluttering.

He stared down at her, his blue eyes burning with a strange yet thrilling light, and her heart began thundering again. He took a deep breath, clenched his hard jaw, looked at her mouth, then muttered, "Ah, what the hell," before he flipped up her veil.

And then he bent his head and kissed her again.

And she kissed him back. With everything in her.

The kiss was rougher than the first, but just as exciting, maybe more so. His mouth expertly plied hers open and his tongue swept inside.

Firecrackers exploded inside of her, hot and bright, showering her body with fiery sparks, creating an ache deep within her.

And the sense of rightness she'd felt during the first kiss came back with a vengeance.

His hands slid from her shoulders around to her back to gather her near, and she went eagerly, needing to burrow as close as she could. She loved the feel of his big, hard body against hers and she adored his mouth on hers, kissing her hard and deep.

He lifted his head and trailed kisses along her jaw to her ear. His rough chin rubbed delightfully against her cheek. "Anna, sweetheart, God you smell good," he rasped in her ear, sending hot tingles down her spine.

His words stoked the blaze in her, turning her already singed insides into pure, molten fire. Just when she thought she would burn up from the inside out, he abruptly jerked away.

Her rubbery legs almost gave out. She pressed her hands back against the wall to steady herself.

He drew in a heavy, ragged breath. "I'm…I'm sorry."

Even though she was still reeling from his kiss, and the hot, wonderful way it had made her feel, a shaft of disappointment traveled through her jumbled emotions to poke at her. "You're sorry you kissed me?" she managed to say.

"Hell, no," he said, swiping a hand over his face. He looked at the ceiling and shook his head. "I'm not sorry I kissed you. I'm sorry I…came after you like that. But I had to know."

"Know what?"

"If it was a fluke."

"A fluke?" She sounded like a parrot.

"I had to know if the first kiss was a fluke."

She shook her head in disbelief. After the two world-altering kisses they'd shared, why did he have to ask the question? Maybe he was as rattled as she was. The last thing she'd expected to discover today was that Ryan's arms felt like a safe, heavenly place.

She met his intense ocean-blue gaze. Electricity jumped through the air. He shook his head.

"It wasn't," he said at the same time she did.

So. They were on the same wavelength. Both of them realized that their kisses weren't any kind of odd coincidence.

He spun on his heel, his mouth thinning, and walked away.

Okay. So he didn't look very happy about their realization. She understood that. She wasn't over-joyed by how much she liked—*loved*—his kisses, ei-ther. She didn't want to like anything about Ryan. She'd never wanted that.

But there it was. The cold, hard truth. Though she'd been fighting it ever since she'd first seen him, though she feared she was stumbling into another mistake, she couldn't ignore what was now obvious.

She was falling for Ryan Cavanaugh.

She sagged back against the wall and pressed a hand to her forehead, wondering when she'd forgotten how important it was to keep her guard up around an exciting man like him.

The stunned, disbelieving look on Anna's face rubbed Ryan the wrong way.

Which was stupid, really. It shouldn't mean any-thing to him one way or another how upset she was about their burn-him-up-from-the-inside kisses not being a fluke. But he always tried not to lie to himself, and he wasn't about to start now.

Her incredulity bugged the hell out of him.

But damn if he didn't understand so well why she was upset. He felt exactly the same way. Stunned. Disbelieving. Floored by how much her kisses af-fected him. As though his blood had been replaced by fire. As though he'd never known lips so soft and compelling. As though he'd found something rare and special.

He paced away, suppressing a snort. After Sonya's betrayal, he wouldn't let any woman ever be special again.

But obviously he was attracted to Anna. No surprise there. She was beautiful and strong and down-to-earth and normal and he enjoyed spending time with her. He admired how determined she was to make her business a success.

And he was tired of fighting his attraction. Damn tired. This…feeling was nothing but old-fashioned lust. Maybe he just needed to spend some time with her to get her out of his system.

He walked back toward her. "You want some dinner?" he asked her, not wanting to waste any time dealing with—and getting rid of—his lust.

She blinked twice. "You want to eat now? Again? You're a bottomless pit."

He shrugged, unwilling to share exactly *why* her assessment was correct. His poverty-ridden past wasn't something he liked to admit to. "Sure. Why don't we go back to my place and I'll make something."

"You cook?"

"On the grill. How do some grilled veggies and disgusting protein substitute sound?"

She smiled. "You mean tofu."

"Yeah." He made a face. "That stuff."

She looked at him for a long moment, and he figured she was probably trying to decide whether to risk spending more time with him. It wasn't too hard to see that she was just as upset by her attraction to him as he was by his to her.

His chest tightened when he thought about that, but he ignored the tugging sensation.

"Are you going to kiss me again?" she asked in a small voice.

*I'd like to kiss you all over.* His thought lit fires all over his body. He took off his jacket. "Maybe. Is that a bad thing?"

"I don't know."

His sentiments exactly. "Let's just see how things go, all right? I won't kiss you unless you want me to."

That didn't seem to reassure her. She walked away then paced back, clenching her hands the whole way. "All right," she finally said. "But it's just dinner. Okay?"

Surprised—and pleased—by her agreement, he said, "Fine with me. Dinner is all I'm interested in." He smiled, ignoring the tiny voice in the back of his brain shouting "liar!"

She smiled back. Sort of. "Good."

Somewhere deep inside of him, in a place he didn't go very often, he was afraid he wanted much more from Anna than just one dinner.

But he wouldn't let himself think about that. Once he spent some time with her and proved to himself that his attraction was just simple lust, he could deal with it and move on.

Because he had to move on. Sonya's cruel betrayal had made sure that he'd never stay put romantically for long.

It didn't take much time for Anna to figure out that Ryan drove like a madman. An in-control, expert-driver kind of madman, but a madman just the same.

He used every bit of considerable horsepower under the hood of his Porsche when he drove from the small market they'd stopped at for dinner supplies to his residence. On more than one occasion, she found herself gripping the granny handle on her door, wishing he would slow down. But, of course, he didn't, and she wasn't surprised. He was the kind of guy who would actually go bungee-jumping for publicity, for goodness sakes. No way was he going to drive his high-octane sports car like a little old lady.

He took a tight curve and the car stuck like glue to the road. The engine revved when he gunned it to accelerate out of the curve. Her stomach, already in knots because of how nervous she was to be alone with him, slid into a tighter bundle.

Ryan downshifted and came to a quick stop in front of a stoplight. He threw her a smile, showing his devastating dimples. "You okay?" He must have noticed her white-knuckling the door handle.

She swallowed, sucked in a breath, and tried to return his smile. "Of course." She wished she had driven her car to the Bridal Show instead of allowing Ryan to pick her up. That way she would have been able to follow him in her own car instead of having to ride with a Mario Andretti clone whose smile snatched away her sanity like a wily thief.

He reached over and put his hand on her knee and gently squeezed.

She jumped.

His hand lingered, burning a hole straight to her skin through the jeans she'd changed into. "Is my driving making you nervous?" He returned his hand to the steering wheel when the light changed. He accelerated quickly, shifting gears like a pro.

*Everything about you makes me nervous.*

"No," she automatically answered in a too-high voice, too distracted by the warm spot his hand had left on her knee. Why, oh why, had she ever agreed to this?

When she thought about it, the reason was obvious. She'd agreed to have dinner with Ryan because she was out and out fascinated by him. She wished she wasn't, but his skin-tingling, blow-up-her-heart, heavenly kisses had revealed her true feelings.

And she couldn't ignore that Ryan seemed to be remarkably concerned about her. He'd offered her an out before the ceremony and he'd reassured her during the ceremony when she'd wanted to bolt.

She sensed something special underneath Ryan's flash and charisma, something that controlled her like the moon did the tides.

She was drawn to him. Tonight would be an excellent opportunity to discover why. As long as she was cautious, everything would be fine. Maybe then she could sort out her feelings for him once and for all.

Maybe then she could tell him the truth about who she really was, a glaring omission that was starting to eat away at her.

Here goes nothing, she thought.

Or everything.

# Chapter Eight

Anna took a deep, calming breath and stepped through the door to Ryan's twentieth floor luxury apartment, her straw tote bag in her hand. Before she had a chance to look around, a black, curly thing came skittering across the polished tile entry and hurled itself at her legs, jumping up and down like a spring masquerading as a dog.

"You have a dog?" she exclaimed, enthralled by the small bundle of fur. She put her bag down and bent down to pet the mutt, who put its paws on her knees and wagged its tail, its hind end moving from side to side with every wag. The fur on its head felt like soft wool.

"Max, down," Ryan commanded. "Sit."

Max ignored the command and remained where he was, his stubby tail wagging, his small body wiggling around in glee as Anna rubbed behind his soft little ears.

Max whined and then stood on his hind legs, pawed the air and barked.

Ryan's face softened. He smiled, shoved his keys into his pocket and set the groceries on the floor. "Yeah, yeah, I know. I like it when she touches me, too." He knelt on the floor and Max sprang into his arms with a hearty yip.

Ryan's statement sent pleasure rocketing through Anna. Grinning, she watched Ryan smother Max with attention, rubbing the dog's back and ears with his big hands. "You like that, don'tcha, girl, oh yes, you do," he murmured.

Anna ignored the yearning to have Ryan's hands on her like they were on Max and focused on the fact that Max had turned out to be a girl instead of a boy.

"I thought *she* was a *he*," she said.

"Most people make that mistake. Max is short for Maxine. Isn't it, honey," he purred, looking down at Max. With Max still in his arms soaking up all of his attention with a thoroughly blissful look on her little doggy face, Ryan stood.

He showered the small bundle of fur with love, and Anna's heart contracted, then expanded until it felt like it was much too big for her chest. To take her mind off of the tightness inside of her, she looked around his apartment.

Straight through the spacious entryway was the living room. A hall led left, probably to the bedrooms, and another led right, where she could see part of the kitchen.

She moved into the living room, stepping onto plush, cream-colored carpet that looked like it had never been walked on. She was surprised to see only three pieces of furniture in the room—a huge, dark leather couch and love seat combination and a big screen TV. A large, ornate glass and marble fireplace dominated the other end of the room. A sea of empty space separated one end of the room from the other.

That was it. There was no other furniture, no accessories and no artwork on the walls. Just an almost bare, impersonal room.

He came up behind her. "I haven't had time to decorate," he said, a note of defensiveness in his voice.

She slid him a speculative glance. "You have time to take care of a dog, but not to decorate?"

"Max is my neighbor's dog. I'm just taking care of her for a few days, right, Maxi?" He scruffed Max's head. "Speaking of which, I need to take her out. Do you want to come with or stay here?"

"I'll stay here," she replied quickly. She needed time to regroup.

Ryan nodded. "Feel free to look around," he said, moving back toward the front door. He grabbed a leash hanging on a hook by the door and carried Max out.

Feeling like she could breathe a little easier with Ryan gone, she looked out the wall of windows, admiring what little she could see of the city, shrouded in gray, misty clouds, then she turned and headed in the direction of the kitchen. She didn't intend on venturing down the hallway toward Ryan's bedroom.

Ryan's bedroom.

A hot flash of fire snaked its way into her stomach and she tried to ignore it. She intended to be cautious and sane tonight, and cautious and sane definitely didn't include Ryan's bed in any way, shape or form.

Refocusing her attention on exploring the safe parts

of his home, she walked under an arched doorway, through the empty dining room to the family room/ kitchen area. The kitchen on the right consisted of lots of modern, chrome-accented appliances. A huge granite island, complete with cooktop, dominated much of the floor space there. An eating area, devoid of a table, occupied one wall.

Strangely, every surface was bare. The room was stark and plain, with no homey touches or decoration. How often did he actually eat here? The kitchen looked like it hadn't ever been used.

She moved into the adjoining family room. The far wall held large, built-in bookcases, which boasted another large TV, a few stacks of books and magazines, and not much else. One lone couch, upholstered in a functional plaid print, sat across from the TV. A dark wooden coffee table strewn with magazines was the only sign she'd seen, apart from Max, that someone actually lived here. No plants. No decorations. No pictures or personalization of any kind.

Her curiosity about Ryan exploded. Was he simply too busy, as he'd said, to decorate? Granted, he'd built a large business on his own. He probably *was* very busy. But this empty, sterile apartment seemed like more than just the home of a busy guy.

It seemed empty. Lonely. Uncared for.

A ribbon of sadness twisted through her. Ryan seemed so put-together and on top of the world, but his apartment, while obviously very luxurious, was devoid of anything attached to *him*. And that almost broke her heart. She wanted to fill his living space with warmth and flowers and things that he'd enjoy.

Looking for a distraction to keep herself from thinking about how she'd warm up Ryan's apartment, among other things, she glanced around and spied a lone, framed picture on one of the bookcase shelves. Curious about why Ryan would have only one picture in his entire house, or at least the parts she'd seen, she rose and walked to the bookcase and picked up the picture.

A little boy of about five or six, with big, brown eyes and black hair stared back at her. He wasn't smiling; in fact he looked kind of sad. The picture looked like a generic school photo, nothing like the fancy portraits her parents had always commissioned.

Who was this boy?

*Ryan's son?*

Another knot building in her, she studied the picture, trying to find some resemblance to Ryan, but there was none. Even so, the child *could* be his son.

With shaking hands she set the picture down. Surely Ryan would have told her if he had a son. Then again, she hadn't been completely honest with him, had she? Maybe the boy was a nephew or child of a friend. She made a mental note to ask Ryan about the child in the picture.

She stepped back and looked up, noticing something protruding from one of the higher shelves. Reaching up, she put her hand on the flat object and slid it off the shelf, noticing that it was another framed picture, which had either fallen down or been put face-down on the shelf.

She looked at the photo and saw a family of three standing in front of Cinderella's Castle at Disneyland. Her gaze immediately went to the lone child, and she knew instantly that the child was Ryan at the age of about ten or eleven. He had a tentative smile on his face, like smiling was tough, but his dimples were obvious and his blue, blue eyes were the same. Even then, he possessed the classic bone structure that hinted at the handsome man he now was.

She focused in on Ryan's mom and dad, curious about the people who'd raised a man like Ryan, remembering he'd told her his parents fought a lot.

His father was a big, hulking man with unkept blond hair. He was smiling, but it bordered on a sneer, and his eyes were dark and flat, not the sparkling blue of his son. He looked like the kind of guy who would rule his household with an iron hand.

Ryan's mother was beautiful, but she, too, looked like smiling was an effort. She had Ryan's dark-blond, golden hair, his dimples, and his blue eyes. But she appeared world-weary and pinched, and it didn't take an expert to figure out that beneath the smiling facade, she wasn't a particularly happy person.

On the surface, the photo looked to be of a happy family on an outing to an amusement park, but under the surface of the happy family, she sensed the familial strife Ryan had hinted at. No one was touching or really smiling genuinely. If it weren't for the family resemblance, she wouldn't have thought they were related at all.

Her heart ached for him even though a photo couldn't begin to tell the real story about a family. She shouldn't jump to conclusions.

But all of those half smiles still pressed on her heart.

"What are you doing?" Ryan snapped from behind her.

She spun around, her heart pounding, her free hand pressed against her chest. "Oh, Lord, Ryan. You startled me."

He walked toward her, his mouth a grim line. He snatched the picture from her. "Where did you find this?" He stared at her with eyes as hard and cold as blue ice.

Gathering her wits, she took a deep breath and willed her heartbeat into a more regular rhythm. "I— I found it there," she said, indicating the shelf with a gesture. "I'm sorry. I didn't mean to snoop." Even though she really hadn't been snooping. He *had* told her to feel free to look around.

She looked at the picture he held in his hands and ventured, "Your family?"

He stepped back. "I guess you could say that," he said, his voice hard and bitter.

Surprised by his cold reply, she searched his face for a clue about how to proceed with this conversation. Obviously his family was a touchy subject. "What do you mean?"

He looked at the photo and pain flashed in his eyes. "This is the only time I can ever remember doing something fun with my parents." He spoke so softly she could barely hear him.

A profound and touching sadness seeped from his words directly into her heart. She touched his arm, hoping to somehow ease his hurt by letting him know she understood it. "I know how you feel—"

He jerked his arm away. "Oh, yeah? Did you ever have to wear shoes with holes in them or clothes that were too small because there wasn't any money for ones that fit?" He snorted. "We only went on that trip to Disneyland because my mom won some money playing bingo." He looked away, his jaw clenched tight. "My parents should have spent the money on food."

She stiffened. Indignant fire burned in her chest, momentarily overriding the heartbreaking, unexpected revelation that Ryan had grown up without enough to eat. No wonder he liked to eat so much now. "You don't know anything about me." She'd made sure of it. "Sure, money wasn't a problem for my family. But that's beside the point. I would have traded every dollar my father had to hear the words 'I love you' from him."

"Money, love," he snapped. "At least you had one of the two."

She looked right into his eyes. "And that makes my father's inability to show his love and respect my dreams okay? I've wanted to be a bridal designer since I attended a wedding when I was ten and was awed by the bride's satin and lace dress. He knew that but pushed aside my dream for his. Are you saying that's okay because I wasn't starving?"

In a heartbeat, he looked stricken. "No, no. That's not what I meant. I mean that at least you didn't have to worry about having enough to eat."

She understood what he was trying to say, and she would give him the benefit of the doubt. She suspected his reasoning was skewed because of his traumatic upbringing. "I'm sure your parents loved you in their own way," she said, hoping for Ryan's sake that they had.

"Don't even go there." Pain flashed in his eyes again. "I was an inconvenience, a mouth to feed, nothing more."

She paused for a long second, wishing she could wipe away the ache so visible in his eyes. But she couldn't. All she could do was offer her understanding and hope that would be enough. "Believe it or not," she said softly, "I know how you feel. I would have given anything for my father to tell me he loved me."

He looked at her and his face softened. He stepped closer and grazed her cheek with a finger. "I guess you do understand, then, don't you?" He searched her face, then zeroed in on her eyes.

She nodded, clinging to his gaze, enjoying the soft brush of his fingers against her skin. "I do."

His masculine scent—a combination of soap and his aftershave—surrounded her, which, along with his touch, warped her senses like a vinyl record left out in the sun. She needed to stay in control tonight, and getting lost in his heavenly smell and crystal-clear blue eyes wasn't the way to do that.

Remembering the photo of the boy, she stepped away and said, "Who's that boy?" She pointed to the photo, bracing herself for not only his possible anger at her prying, but also for his explanation. That boy could be his son.

To her relief, he grinned, but she still held her breath. "That's Juan. He's my little brother."

She let out her breath and frowned. "You have a brother that young?"

"Not my *real* little brother. One from the Mentor A Child foundation."

A shaft of surprised admiration bolted through her. "You actually take time out of your busy schedule to help that little boy?"

"Surprised?" he said, the hard note back in his voice. "I do more than just raise money for the foundation, you know. Why do you find that so hard to believe?"

She held up a hand. "I don't," she said, which a

few days ago would have been a lie. "You just seem like such a busy person, I was surprised you had time to really get that involved with the organization, that's all." She'd thought he just donated money rather than his time, like her father did.

"I *am* busy," he said, heading toward the foyer. "But I know from personal experience how some kids need an adult in their lives who gives a damn."

Anna stayed put, thinking about what he'd said, feeling incredibly sad that he obviously hadn't had a caring adult in *his* life.

Along with the sadness, though, was a hearty dose of admiration. Ryan was turning out to be so much different than she'd imagined.

So much more dangerous.

"Maxine!" Ryan scolded from the entryway, cutting off her ominous thoughts.

"What happened?"

Ryan stepped into view with Max perched in his arms. The silly little fluff-ball had a carrot clamped in her teeth, and Anna could have sworn the mutt was smiling.

"Max likes vegetables," he said, turning around to look at the floor behind him. "A lot."

Pressing a hand to her lips, Anna moved forward. Ryan stepped aside, revealing the grocery bag had been knocked over. Half-chewed vegetables lay all over the floor.

Anna looked at Ryan, grinning. "She's a vegetarian, then?"

"I guess so."

She met his mirth-filled eyes. Unable to help herself, she began to laugh. Ryan chuckled and pried the mangled carrot from Max's mouth. "Looks like our vegetable selection is limited now."

She waved a hand in the air. "I don't mind at all."

Ryan put Max on the floor and began cleaning up the mess. Anna squatted next to him and helped, thoroughly amused. Max watched, then gingerly leaned in and snatched a stalk of celery and skulked off with it, presumably to eat in private.

When everything was reloaded into the bags, Anna followed Ryan into the kitchen. He began to unload the groceries, and Anna held back, still reeling from what she'd discovered about Ryan's childhood and his touching involvement with Juan. She watched him putter around the kitchen, liking that he was unfazed by the fact that a naughty dog had almost ruined their dinner.

She remembered what he'd said about her having a hard time believing he was a nice, selfless kind of guy. Boy, did she wish Ryan's suddenly evident selflessness *was* impossible to believe. Then she could pass him off as the shallow, self-centered schemer she'd initially pegged him as and she could walk away from him and never look back.

But now…well, now, as she slowly learned more about him, he was evolving before her eyes into a caring, complex man who hid the pain of a wounded childhood behind a winning smile and helped a little boy grow into a healthy, emotionally complete man.

And what a kisser!

Without warning, her heart pulsed with an emotion she had never, ever felt before. She knew deep inside that she could easily care about the man in the kitchen.

Swiping a shaking hand over her face, she wan-

dered back into the family room, trying to sort out
her feelings. She didn't want to want Ryan, but darn
it, she did. How was she supposed to fight him when
he obliterated her common sense and the walls she'd
built around her heart with kind words and gestures
to a dog, for heaven sake?

She had absolutely no idea.

As he unloaded the groceries in the kitchen, Ryan
slanted several glances at Anna standing like a statue
in the middle of his family room, looking shell-
shocked.

Yeah, his past was pretty ugly, which was why he
usually avoided talking about his twisted family.
Sonya had always made it seem like he was somehow
responsible for his parents' neglect and had berated
him for letting it bother him when it was over and
done with. The shame of his childhood had almost
choked him when he'd been with her, and his childhood was one thing he never wanted to experience
again.

But Anna hadn't blamed him. After talking with
her, he sensed an empathy in her that touched him to
the core and broke down a self-made barrier inside of
him, leaving a portion of his heart unprotected. He
felt connected to her in a way he'd never felt connected to anyone else. She was different. She wasn't
some rich-girl-princess. She was a hardworking
woman who had more in common with him than
Sonya ever had. She was normal. Down-to-earth.

Before he could move forward with his thoughts,
he heard Anna's cell phone ring. She answered and
began to talk, her voice carrying to him in muted
tones.

He stood motionless in the middle of the kitchen, a bag of salvaged red peppers in his hands, returning to his thoughts of Anna. It would be really easy to push her away, wave goodbye and cut out if he didn't feel so damn connected to her. She'd had a rough time of it with her father, too, and had doubted his love her entire life, just as he'd doubted his parents' love.

And, of course, he couldn't ignore his overwhelming physical attraction to her. The mere thought of the kisses they'd shared sent heat and need shooting through his body like a Roman candle.

But her understanding and empathy, combined with his admiration and attraction, might make it hard to keep her out of his heart. And he didn't want another woman anywhere near that part of him ever again.

The thought of opening himself up to the kind of pain and betrayal that had been hard-heartedly handed out to him cooled the heat in his blood. He simply couldn't allow Anna to get too close. He could deal with his physical attraction to her, but he couldn't deal with what she might do to him emotionally.

"Ryan, what's wrong?" Anna softly asked from behind him.

He swung around, jolted out of his thoughts. "Uh, nothing." He threw the bag of peppers on the counter, then reached into the grocery bag and took out an untouched box of mushrooms.

She stepped closer, cocked her head to the side and put her cell phone on the counter. "You look like something's bothering you." She moved in, nearer still, and looked up at him with those big, soft, topaz-hued eyes. "Do you want to talk about it?"

He set the mushrooms on the counter next to the

peppers and roamed his gaze over her stunning face, framed by her dark auburn, shiny hair flowing loose around her shoulders. She was so close and so incredibly beautiful. Her sweet, floral scent wafted over him, relighting the fire that had been smoldering in his blood since he'd kissed her at the bridal show. He wanted to take her in his arms and bury his nose in the sweet-scented skin of her neck and kiss his way to her mouth.

*Why not?* What he was feeling was old-fashioned lust, and he was capable of dealing with *that.* They were both adults, and she *had* agreed to come here with him. He sensed an answering attraction in her, and she certainly hadn't seemed to mind their second kiss at the bridal show.

He snaked an arm out and reeled her against his body. He swooped his head down and pressed his mouth to her neck just beneath her jaw. "No, I don't want to talk," he murmured against her scented skin. He eased back and looked at her, intending to honor his word and only kiss her if she wanted him to. "Is it all right if I kiss you?"

Wide-eyed, she stared at him, then nodded.

His heart pounding, he buried his mouth beneath her jaw again. And then he kissed his way quickly to her mouth, wanting to linger on her soft, smooth skin but wanting his lips on hers more.

She gave a breathy little gasp, wrapped her arms around his neck and pushed against him. He devoured her mouth, deepening the kiss, wanting to feel her tongue moving against his.

Even though she was plastered against him from shoulder to thigh, he wanted her closer. He skimmed his hand down her slim back to her firm, curvy bottom and cupped the toned flesh in his hands, then pulled her hips up and in, nestling himself against the warm juncture of her thighs.

She met his kiss with a passion that fueled the inferno in his blood to an even higher level. She was so soft and warm and wonderful in his arms. Needing to feel every inch of her, he moved his upper body away just enough to cup her breast in his hand.

He caressed her fullness gently through her T-shirt. Fresh sparks skidded along every nerve ending in his body. But touching her through her clothing wasn't enough. He wanted to feel her naked skin. As he continued to ply her soft mouth with deep, drugging kisses, he eased her shirt up and burrowed his hand beneath until he encountered the delicate lace of her bra.

She jerked away with a muted cry.

He snapped his head up, fighting to shift gears. He instinctively reached for her. "Anna." His hands gripped her shoulders. "Come back here."

She parted her rosy lips and shook her head slowly, her eyes wide, then dropped her head against his chest. "Ryan, this is all happening too fast for me. We need to slow down."

He dragged in a heavy breath. Through a lust-induced haze, he managed to figure out she was probably right. They were speeding along a road he wasn't sure he wanted to travel. But man, with her soft, sexy body pressed against his, her kisses still burning on his lips, it was damn hard to slow things down.

He would, though, if that was what she wanted, and really, he wanted to get back under control, too. He had to keep things simple between them, and diving headfirst into a physical relationship might just complicate his life. He'd thought he could deal with his red-blooded male lust, but Anna had blown his mind right off the bat. He sure hadn't expected a total meltdown.

He wrapped his arms around her to simply hold her trembling body close, breathe in her wonderful scent and feel her heart beating in time with his. Had he made a tactical error? Obviously Anna affected him deeply in lots and lots of ways, physically as well as emotionally, which he hadn't really expected.

Just like Sonya had.

No. Anna was nothing like any other woman he'd ever known. She was normal. Real. Hardworking. Dedicated.

He wasn't about to give up the heaven he'd found simply holding her in his arms. They would take things slow and easy. He just wasn't ready to walk away from her yet.

*You're getting in too deep, bud.*

Nah, he wasn't. He had everything under control. He knew exactly what he was doing.

Feeling better, he pressed a kiss to Anna's soft, sweet-scented hair, held her tighter and lost himself in the wonderful way she made him feel.

And he did his best to ignore the unrelenting voice in the back of his head screaming a warning.

## Chapter Nine

The next day, before her next meeting with Mr. Lewis of Perfect Bridal, Anna called Ryan to be sure he would be home. She then drove to his apartment to retrieve her cell phone, which she'd inadvertently left the night before, on the way to the rental car office. The car she'd rented wasn't starting correctly and she'd arranged to pick up another vehicle.

Actually, she probably could have waited to call Ryan until later in the day, or until tomorrow, but she wanted to see him, wanted to enjoy his smile and dazzling blue eyes and the blissful way he always made her feel *right now*.

Though it was drizzling from a leaden sky and the day was on the chilly side, she couldn't help but smile as she pulled into a guest parking spot in his apartment building's parking area. Her heart felt light and buoyant and a deep, telling happiness had descended around her.

Being with Ryan last night, feeling his strong arms

around her, hearing him whisper and laugh in her ear while they'd watched a sitcom cuddled up on the couch in his family room, Max snuggled between them, had been sheer heaven to her wounded soul. Ryan had been attentive, solicitous and so darn attractive it was all she could do not to let herself want him forever.

He was turning into a man who would be so very easy to care about, despite the doubts other men had carved into her heart, doubts that cut so sharply she wasn't sure she would ever be able to forget them.

Equally as disturbing was the notion that Ryan still thought of her as simply Anna Simpson. He had no idea who she really was or that she was an heiress to an enormous fortune. Was it time to tell him the truth? Surely he would keep her secret.

Wouldn't he?

That tiny grain of doubt dug deep. Too many scheming men had taken advantage of Anna Sinclair for her to reveal her true identity to Ryan just yet. But she would. Soon.

Wanting back the wonderful mood she'd been in, something that had been missing in her life of late, she refocused on the here and now, ignoring the words that had been circling in her brain all morning.

*How did I let this happen?*

She steadfastly ignored the question as she parked her car and made her way to Ryan's apartment via the elevator, her heart dancing a two-step in her chest even though she was sailing into dangerous waters.

She hesitated outside his door, making the effort to calm the telltale giddiness skipping through her. She smoothed the straight skirt of her basic black business ensemble and then lifted her hand and rapped on the door.

Ryan answered. "Anna." His handsome face bloomed into a wide, genuine smile, and he looked as happy to see her as she was to see him.

Even though she knew she was a fool to be so darn ecstatic to see him, she smiled shakily, happiness brimming inside of her, trying not to stare, feeling a wave of pure yearning move through her. As she would expect, he looked as handsome as ever, though different. Instead of his usual business attire, he wore jeans and a tight black T-shirt that hugged his body like a second skin and accentuated his tan face, golden hair and pearly white teeth.

And he had a small boy attached to his leg.

Juan.

"Hi," she said to Ryan. She smiled and waved at Juan peeking out at her with big, brown eyes from in back of Ryan. "Hi there."

Juan hid his face behind Ryan.

Ryan turned and looked down. "Hey, buddy. Do you want to meet a friend of mine?"

The boy shook his head.

"Feeling a little shy?" Ryan asked him.

His eyes wide, Juan nodded.

Ryan held up his index finger to Anna. "Just a second." He hunkered down so he was on the boy's level. "You want me to hold you?"

Juan nodded again, and then leaned forward and buried his face against Ryan's neck. Ryan put his big arms around the boy and squeezed tight. He whispered something in Juan's ear. Juan giggled, then Ryan lifted him up and settled him tightly against himself.

The sight of Juan's small body enfolded in Ryan's bulging, muscular-yet-gentle arms knocked the breath right out of her. A knot slid tight in her chest, and she struggled to draw a breath. She'd never expected him to be capable of such tenderness, such unselfish caring.

Warning sirens went off in her head.

Ryan stood and swiveled toward her. "Come on in. I'll get your phone."

She nodded, unable to speak around the unanticipated lump of emotion in her throat, and waited in the foyer for Ryan.

Her untrustworthy guard shifted down, collapsing under the onslaught of this compelling, wonderful Ryan. Little by little, she'd been falling further under his spell ever since they'd talked the night before and she'd had a glimpse of the genuine man beneath the polished, smooth exterior. Ryan had become a real man to her in the last twenty-four hours, a person who'd risen from a painful childhood. A man who did more than simply write a check to his favorite charity, one who took care of cute dogs and needy children.

At this moment, seeing him with Juan, Ryan's unlikely transformation had become astoundingly complete.

He was a man she could care about.

A wave of heady anticipation rolled through her, creating goose bumps under her skin and a flutter in her heart, only to be doused by reality.

*Oh, boy. I'm getting in over my head.*

Before she could consider that worrying thought, Ryan returned, her phone in one hand, Juan still perched in his arms. "Look, I'm sorry I can't ask you to stay. I have a meeting in Lake Oswego in an hour and I was just on my way out to take Juan home.'' He reached out and touched her cheek. ''Want to walk out with us?''

She nodded, the spot he'd touched on her cheek blazing.

They rode the elevator down in silence, stopping at each floor, Ryan explained, so Juan could practice counting backward. It was obvious Juan was behind on his counting skills. He made a lot of mistakes. But Ryan had infinite patience with the boy, gently whispering clues, helping him figure out what number came next without making Juan feel as if he'd made an error.

It was all Anna could do to keep her eyes focused straight ahead rather than on how sweet Ryan looked with the adoring child nestled close, looking up at Ryan for guidance, his big brown eyes filled with love and trust. Clearly Juan and Ryan had a strong bond, and Anna found herself touched and fascinated. How many single men would take the time to reach out to a needy child?

They walked in silence to the parking lot. Ryan waited as she climbed into her car. She turned the key in the ignition—and nothing happened.

Ryan tapped on her window and she rolled it down. ''Problem?'' he asked.

''I hope not.'' She tried the ignition again. No luck. The car wouldn't even turn over this time. She slumped down in her seat, wishing she'd gone to the car rental agency *before* she'd come here.

Ryan leaned down. ''Car not working?''

''Yes. It's been giving me problems, and I was on my way to take it in.''

"Need a ride somewhere?"

She checked her watch. Her meeting with Mr. Lewis started in half an hour. She didn't have time to catch a bus or wait for a taxi. She grabbed her bag. "I guess I do."

"I have to take Juan home first. He lives fairly close. Is that okay?"

"Sure." She exited the car and followed them to Ryan's car.

"Looks like you've got a lemon there." He pointed back to her car. "I'll take care of it when I get home, all right?"

"I've already made arrangements to trade it in for another car."

He opened the car door for her. "I'll do that for you."

Her heart warmed by his thoughtfulness (darn, why did he keep doing that?), she nodded and settled next to Ryan after he hooked Juan into a car seat in the back of a late model Volvo sedan she hadn't even known Ryan owned.

"Why do you have two cars?" she asked.

Ryan drove out of the parking garage. "Juan can't ride in my Porsche because of the airbag, so I bought this."

"You bought a different car because of Juan?"

He looked at her and pulled a face. "Of course I did. I see him a couple of times a week. I had to have a car for him to ride in."

Her heart rolled over in her chest, smashing the fence around it flat.

"Contrary to what you seem to believe," Ryan said when they stopped at a stop sign. "I am a nice guy, you know."

Oh, after seeing him with Juan, she was beginning to believe it, all right. He *was* a nice guy, a wonderful one.

Maybe too wonderful for her to resist.

She sat in stunned silence for the few minutes it took to reach Juan's apartment.

Juan's home turned out to be a wretched, run-down multi-story apartment complex in the heart of the city. Garbage littered the sidewalk near the entrance and many of the windows were either boarded up or barred. Traffic rushed by, billowing exhaust and dust, and she noticed several transients hanging out in the small, shabby entryway.

Appalled, she turned wide eyes toward Ryan and shook her head slightly. He simply nodded his understanding.

She waved goodbye to Juan and Ryan got out of the car, opened the back door and helped the boy from his car seat. Anna noticed the seat stayed in the car. Ryan probably owned it.

An elderly, gray-haired, stooped woman shuffled forward to greet Juan. She smiled toothlessly at Ryan, who put a hand on her shoulder before he reached into his pocket and took out his wallet. He peeled off several bills and tried to hand them to the old woman. She eyed the money, then hesitantly took it with the good grace of someone who knew that she had to stuff her pride for Juan's sake.

Ryan squatted down and took a now crying Juan into his arms and gave him a good, long bear hug. He then gently wiped the tears from the sobbing boy's cheeks and said something. Juan nodded woefully, then threw himself into Ryan arms, clinging to his broad shoulders with his skinny arms.

Anna turned away, tears stinging her eyes, and pressed a shaking hand to her lips.

*Oh, Ryan. Is your heart breaking like mine?*

She turned away from the touching scene unfolding before her, wishing Ryan had turned out to be as shallow as she'd originally thought him to be. She needed to keep her distance, and keeping her distance from a loving, tenderhearted man like him was proving to be almost impossible.

She shifted uncomfortably on the leather seat.

After what seemed like a long time, Ryan climbed back into the car. He sat for a moment, his hands clenched on the steering wheel, saying nothing. Finally he said, "God, I hate taking him back to that dump."

Anna sniffed. "Is that his grandmother?"

"Yeah, and she tries hard. But Juan's parents are drug addicts and are both in jail, and she has no money and no job. I help out as best I can, but she's too stubborn and proud to let me do more. I'm trying to convince her to let me move them, but she says this is her home."

She stared at him, deeply moved by what he was doing for Juan. "You love him, don't you?"

He eased out into traffic, keeping his eyes on the road, then lifted one large shoulder and let it fall. "Yeah, I do."

She stared at his profile, one brow lifted. "Weren't you the guy who told me love doesn't exist?"

He glanced at her. "Loving a child is different."

She quickly looked away and gazed out the window, an ache beginning to take root in her chest. "What do you mean?"

He pressed his mouth into a grim line. "I guess I meant that *romantic* love doesn't exist."

Slowly the ache that had begun to grow in her spread its roots throughout her body, numbing her from the inside out. He'd stated the unvarnished truth again, verbalized so even a fool could figure it out. Ryan could love Juan, but not a woman.

He couldn't love her.

She fought back sudden, hot, ridiculous tears. "You're so darn stubborn, you can't even admit the truth to yourself, can you?"

"What do you mean?" he asked, his tone tight.

"You still carry the scars of your childhood, and that colors everything you do."

He held up a hand. "No way. You're overanalyzing my life. I like things simple, that's all."

Her shoulders slumped. Obviously he wasn't ready to face the reality that his inability to admit romantic love existed was tied directly to the love he'd never had.

He downshifted and stopped at a light, then turned and looked at her, but she stared straight ahead, not wanting him to see the moisture in her eyes.

"And what about you, Anna? What about the doubt you've been living on since who-knows-when?"

She pulled her eyebrows together. "What doubt?"

He laughed under his breath. "The doubt that won't allow you to trust me. I think I've proven myself to be a pretty decent guy. I'd appreciate a little slack, okay? Not everybody is out to get you."

She threw him a stiff glance. "I don't think that."

"Oh, come on, honey. You've been expecting me to take advantage of you or hurt you since the day we met.'' He made a quick left. ''Are you going to go through life shutting people out because you're afraid they'll hurt you?''

She lifted a brow. ''Shutting people out like you do?''

He stomped on the brakes and pulled over to the curb. ''I don't do that.''

''Yes, you do. You're afraid to love anybody because your parents didn't love you. It's the same thing.''

He sat silently, then shook his head. ''No, it's not. I don't believe in love, period—oh, okay, I do believe in loving Juan, but that's as far as it goes. You design *wedding dresses,* for heaven sake, and yet you still deny love exists. Now who's lying to herself?''

Her brain twisted into a huge wad of confused thoughts. His words made sense on one level, but on a deeper, more emotional level she was still so afraid to believe in love beyond taking silk, satin and pearls and creating a dream gown for a bride.

She sat, frozen, unable to summon a response.

''Anna, look at me.''

She slowly turned toward him. His eyes turned to a soft, worn-denim blue. He reached out and drifted his fingers across her cheek. ''I'm sorry if I've upset you.'' He leaned close and kissed her softly, his lips as gentle and tender as the fluttering of a butterfly's wings. His scent engulfed her, lulling her senses. He wrapped his strong, capable arms around her and she felt safe and complete. ''I never meant to make you sad,'' he whispered, his voice low and husky.

She should heed the lessons in her past and pull away. But she couldn't muster the strength to resist him. A now familiar sense of utter belonging settled down around her like a tangle of flowering vines, wrapping her in a feeling she had never, *ever* experienced before.

How in the world could she fight him?

As he eased her closer, kissing her until she didn't know where she ended and he started, she wasn't sure she wanted to try any more.

Somewhere in the very back of her mind, a tiny voice told her it wasn't that simple, that letting herself believe that Ryan might love her was foolish.

She hadn't told him who she really was.

She would be leaving in a few days.

He'd been very clear that he didn't believe in romantic love.

She didn't want to take the risk love demanded.

But she ignored the voice and all of her doubts and nagging worries, unable to focus on anything but Ryan pressed against her, his arms holding her against his heart. She kissed him back with everything in her, feeling bliss and contentment steal through her one heartbeat at a time.

And everything else faded away.

Except for the tiniest grain of black doubt in her heart.

"Oh, my stars," Anna uttered. She reread the headline in the newspaper she'd come across in the lobby of her hotel the morning after she'd kissed Ryan in his car, not quite believing what it said.

But there it was, in black and white, although from her viewpoint the headline might as well be written in glaring neon letters that would shine all over the world.

Anna Sinclair, Philadelphia Heiress, Masquerading As Bridal Designer Anna Simpson In *The Bridal Chronicles*

Horrified, she pressed a shaky hand over her mouth and started to read the story. It went on to describe that the woman who had posed as the happy bride to Ryan Cavanaugh, the wealthy owner of Java Joint, was really socialite Anna Sinclair from Philadelphia, daughter of one of the richest men in America, banking baron Peter Sinclair.

She crumpled the paper, unable to read the whole thing, and took off her dark glasses—did she really need them now?—gave into her shaking knees and sank down onto a couch in the hotel lobby, her stomach twisting. How had this happened? Nobody in Portland knew who she really was, and she'd been so very careful, except when she'd rushed down to the lobby without her hat and glasses...

The dry cleaner deliveryman.

Of course! He'd leaked the story. She should have suspected a story was in the works when she'd seen that reporter at the Bridal Show. She looked around, suddenly even more paranoid of the people around her than she'd been in the past, half expecting some tabloid reporter to materialize out of thin air in front of her.

Darn it all. Trust things to explode in her face when her life was finally coming together. Her meeting with Mr. Lewis yesterday had gone extremely well, and she felt that he was close to signing an agreement with her. She had another meeting with him in a little over an hour.

She pressed a hand to her mouth. Dear heaven,

Ryan would discover her true identity along with the rest of the world! He would know then that she'd lied to him, that she'd let him believe that she was simply modest working girl Anna Simpson rather than the heiress to a huge banking fortune she really was. That was an extremely huge omission on her part, one that she wished she'd rectified sooner but had never found the right moment to do so.

Ryan might never forgive her for her deceit. And that mattered because…?

A hot chill swirled through her.

She was falling in love with him.

Despite how hard she'd tried to keep him at a distance and to keep herself from becoming involved with a man after her painful experiences, he'd crept into her heart anyway.

How did she let this happen? How could she let her guard down so easily?

Deeply confused and shocked by her feelings for Ryan, she shook her head, unable to comprehend how easily she'd let a man close enough to hurt her.

Disgusted with herself, she glanced up and saw a man with long dark hair and glasses heading toward her, a notepad in hand.

The press.

Her heart sank. Real life once again. Funny how that always managed to intrude at the absolute worst moment.

"Anna Simpson?" he called, stalking closer. "Or should I be calling you Miss Sinclair?"

The reporter's gall sent fresh, hot indignation ripping through her, galvanizing her into action. She put her dark glasses back on, shot to her feet, jammed the newspaper into her straw tote bag, threw the bag's handle over her shoulder and ran.

"Wait!" he shouted. "I have a few questions!"

Her heart racing, she ignored him. Without looking back, she kept running, across the marble floor of the lobby, then out the door of the hotel toward the parking lot where she'd parked her car.

She reached her car in record time, thankful that Ryan had kept his promise and had been considerate enough to have the rental agency deliver a working vehicle last night. She opened the door and flung her bag onto the front passenger seat. She quickly sat, inserted the key and turned the ignition, quickly heading out of the parking lot.

As she drove with no particular destination in mind, the truth bored in on her. The story in the newspaper had forced her hand. She had to tell Ryan the truth.

Even if he hated her for lying to him about something as important as her real identity.

The thought of Ryan hating her twisted her stomach into a painful knot. Her hands gripping the steering wheel, she headed in the direction of his office, trying not to think about losing him and what that would mean to her. Even though she was a fool to care whether she lost Ryan or not, she simply wasn't ready to go down that path yet.

She refused to consider why.

Fifteen minutes later, she drove into the parking structure beneath his office and saw his Porsche parked in its spot near the elevator.

She parked and took a deep breath, willing herself to calm down and deal with her mistake. Hopefully Ryan would accept her incredibly belated honesty. A few minutes later she stepped out of the elevator and forced herself to walk down the hall to Ryan's office, giving the receptionist a feeble wave as she walked by the front desk.

The door to Ryan's office stood wide open. Anna pressed herself against the wall, chewing on her lip, working up her courage to do what had to be done.

Plastering a smile on her face, she poked her head around the jamb and saw Ryan at his desk typing on a laptop, his dark golden head bent in deep concentration. He wore a snowy-white dress shirt and colorful tie loosened around his neck.

She wiped her damp palms on her jeans. Her stomach fluttered like it always did when she came near him, and she was struck almost dumb by his blatant male beauty. "Hello?" she quavered. "Anybody home?"

His head popped up, his blue eyes narrowed slightly for a moment as though he resented being interrupted. Just as quickly, mild surprise lit his features and then he flashed the brilliant smile that always made her feel weak in the knees. "Anna." He quickly stood and moved out from behind his desk. "What a nice surprise."

She let out a breath she hadn't realized she'd been holding. Good. He hadn't seen the story yet. Even with that encouraging sign, she was barely able to look him in the eye and return his smile.

Because the news she was about to deliver was going to ensure that her unexpected appearance here wasn't going to be a *nice* surprise for long.

If she were sane, that would be fine. But considering she'd lost whatever shred of sensibility she might have by letting Ryan matter to her, it didn't please her at all.

It simply depressed the heck out of her.

A burst of pure, unadulterated pleasure blasted through Ryan when he saw Anna standing in the door to his office, a tentative smile on her lovely face. Good Lord, who would have expected that he would be so happy to simply have a woman unexpectedly drop by his office?

But he *was* happy to see her. Ecstatic, even. He'd been counting the hours until he could be with her again, looking forward to the evening they'd planned to spend watching videos with an almost unreal amount of anticipation.

Acting on pure instinct, he walked across his office toward her, unable to resist the pull he always felt when she was around. He took her hand and drew her close, simply wanting to hold her in his arms again, feel her heart beating next to his and smell her softly scented skin. He reveled in the knowledge that he'd found a woman like Anna, a woman who was exactly what she seemed, exactly what he needed.

Unpretentious.

Both feet planted firmly on the ground.

Dedicated and hardworking.

*I love her.*

The truth detonated inside of Ryan like a bomb. And as much as he wanted to deny the surprising and unexpected thought, he couldn't. Even though he'd steadfastly believed that romantic love didn't exist, his world had somehow twisted around and he loved Anna more than he ever thought possible.

His heart almost shaking with love for her, a deep,

telling, satisfying sense of pure happiness falling down around him, he pulled away to look at her face, hoping to see his newfound, miraculous love reflected in her pretty brown eyes.

Instead he saw ominous shadows lurking in the depths of her troubled, darkening gaze.

He lowered his brows, ignoring the niggling sense of unease moving through him. "Hey," he said, cupping her chin with his hand, trying to catch her eye. "What's wrong?"

Her eyes dull, she moved toward the couch. "I have something to tell you."

Cold, razor-sharp dread cut through him. *That* sure as hell didn't sound good. "Okay, go ahead." He steeled himself for the agonizing truth—*Ryan, I don't want to see you anymore*—or some Dear Poor Little Ryan line he'd heard before.

Instead of uttering those words, or any words, she simply reached into the tote bag and took out a newspaper. She silently held the paper out to him, looking at the floor, her hand shaking. Damn. She looked like she'd been caught copying someone else's bridal designs.

He reached for the paper. Something was very wrong, but he couldn't imagine what it was. Something about her father? Something about "The Bridal Chronicles?" What?

He clenched his jaw and opened the folded, wrinkled paper.

And saw the headline.

His cold foreboding freezing into a mantle of pure ice, he read the story that told him the sordid, astonishing, kick-him-in-the-teeth-again truth.

Anna Simpson was really some rich woman named Anna Sinclair.

His heart crumbling, he slowly looked up at her, hoping she'd deny that the story was true, tell him that it was just a big, fat, really bad joke. A mistake.

But the truth was plain to see in her suddenly glassy eyes and the stricken, guilty look written all over her face. This was no mistake. No. The story was correct.

She wasn't your normal, hardworking, down-to-earth woman. She was an *heiress* for criminy sakes, the only child of one of the richest men in the entire country!

She was a rich princess who had merrily led him down the garden path.

And that familiar path was a terrible, hurt-filled place he'd vowed never, ever to go down again.

"Why?" was all he could manage to say.

"My father—"

"I know that part," he snapped. He swiped a hand through his hair, then drilled her with a rock-hard look. "I want to know why didn't you tell *me* who you really were."

She bit her lip. "I was going to but—"

"But you didn't until you knew you'd be busted anyway." He slapped the newspaper against his thigh and stalked closer, a cold fire blazing to life in his chest. "Why didn't you tell me sooner?"

"I wasn't sure, until very recently, that I could trust you."

Her doubting his integrity hurt. "Why the hell not? Have I ever given you reason not to trust me?"

Sudden heat burned in her eyes. "You haven't, no. But many other men have. Men who only wanted me because of who I was. Men who used me to get to my money or wheedle their way into my family to get to my father, men who I trusted and then hurt me.''

Horrified, he stared at her and asked, ''Men have actually done those things to you?''

She moved closer, nodding. ''Every man I've ever trusted has betrayed me.''

Ryan fought the sympathy moving through him, needing to stay focused on what she'd done, how she'd played him for a trusting fool. ''So because of all of these other men, you lied to me.''

She simply looked at him for a long, dark moment, then nodded. ''Partly. But I also wanted to keep my identity a secret because I wanted to succeed on my own rather than as Anna Sinclair, Peter Sinclair's daughter.''

He stared at her, thoughts racing through his brain while he tried to absorb the awful truth.

Not down-to-earth, normal Anna.

Rich.

Like Sonya.

Betrayal.

Pain.

And even though he might be able to consider forgiving her for lying, the nail in the coffin holding his dying dreams was one jagged, slicing piece of crucial information:

She was exactly the kind of woman he loathed—a rich, snooty princess who stepped on and lied to others to get what she wanted.

Anger knifed through his heart.

The truth was bitter, and he hated that he'd set himself up—again—for this kind of heartache. Numb with pain, he said, "I think you'd better leave." He walked over to his desk and sat down, staring unseeingly at the computer screen in front of him, deliberately keeping his eyes off of her.

Anna was silent for a long moment. "Ryan, I'm sorry. I thought I was doing the right thing."

"Don't worry about it," he said, his tone deliberately icy. Uncaring. He looked up and stared right into her eyes to make his point. "It doesn't matter." He wouldn't let it.

She stared back, her lips quivering, her eyes filling with tears. "You're not going to forgive me, are you?" Her voice cracked and she sounded very lost and alone.

He quelled his stupid urge to comfort her. "I've been burned too many times by women like you."

"What do you mean, 'women like me'?" She stepped closer, her scent coming with her.

He steeled himself to ignore the wonderful way she smelled, the memories it evoked, and gripped the edge of the desk and rose.

"Tell me," she demanded.

He stood, then stalked out from behind his desk and ran an impatient hand through his hair, moving over to stare out the window, unseeing. "Rich, snooty princesses who walk all over people they deem below them." The minute the words left his mouth, he realized how cold and hard they sounded, how hurtful they might be to her.

For a moment, she looked as if he'd struck her. A sick feeling moved through him and he wished he'd tempered his words a bit.

After she stared at him for a long time, the slow fire burned in her eyes again. She came over to stand next to him. "Just for the record, I never, ever thought you were below me, Ryan. I may be wealthy, but I wasn't raised to think I was better than anybody else because of it. My mother made sure of it."

"That may be true," he said, scoffing. "But nothing can change the fact that you couldn't trust me enough to tell me the truth, right?"

His words hung in the air like thick, acrid smoke, nearly choking the life from him. But, no, it wasn't his words that had sucked him dry. Anna *Sinclair* had done that to him all by herself.

She touched his arm. "That's right. I have my demons, too, demons that color what I do, the decisions I make. Maybe we both need to forget the past and simply think about the future."

He looked at her small hand on his arm and felt her warmth through his shirt. Damn, he wished he could snap his fingers and forget who she was, wished he could think about a future with her. But he couldn't. Cold, bleak reality—the reality she'd dumped on him like a truckload of concrete—wouldn't let him.

"It's not that easy, Anna. You lied to me because of your past. So be it. And while I might be able to forgive a lie, *my* past makes it impossible for me to overlook that you're the kind of woman I can't let myself…be involved with. The past cuts both ways."

She withdrew her shaking hand, clamped her lips together, still staring at him with those glimmering yet sad brown eyes. Finally she stepped back and nodded stiffly. "Fine. I guess I can't argue with that." She moved toward the door, her shoulders rigid, and turned and stared at him for a few seconds.

He quickly looked down.

"I have a meeting with the president of Perfect Bridal in half an hour. I should find out whether I'm going to land the account, so I'll be leaving Portland soon."

She paused and, damn, he wanted to ask her to stay. But he couldn't. Her deception and the woman she'd proven herself to be had seen to that.

And then, before he could reply, she simply said, "Goodbye, Ryan." The next moment the doorway stood empty.

He stood in his office, his chest twisting as an agonizing silence engulfed him, a silence that rang through his suddenly empty, aching heart like a death knell.

The death of his "love" for Anna Simpson.

*Fool.* Anna Simpson was just a fantasy, and so was the love he'd conjured up from some stupid place inside of him, a place that had somehow forgotten that love didn't exist.

He should feel good. He'd done what he'd had to do, what was necessary, what was best.

He'd done what he'd known he should do since Anna Simpson had reeled him in and made him care.

He'd discovered the horrible truth about her.

His heart would stay safe. Whole. Complete.

Strange that he'd never felt so alone in his life.

# *Chapter Ten*

After her third meeting with Mr. Lewis, Anna returned to her hotel. Thankfully he hadn't mentioned the story in the newspaper and had told her that after much consideration, and numerous meetings, he'd decided that he liked the freshness of her designs.

He'd awarded her the account.

The plan had worked. Her business, her dream, was sure to flourish. Now that she had the Perfect Bridal account, she would be able to make the necessary profit required by her father and she could get on with being a successful, well-respected bridal designer. She should be jubilant. Ecstatic. Relieved.

But she wasn't any of those things. As she walked across the lobby, thinking about what had happened at Ryan's office just two hours ago, her heart weeping, a paralyzing, depressing numbness descended over her, obliterating any sense of accomplishment and joy about her business success she should feel.

She'd lied and was paying the ultimate price for that betrayal.

Wishing she'd been able to see past her ridiculous need to conceal her real identity long enough to be honest with Ryan from the beginning, she scurried through the lobby, her hat shoved down on her head, her dark glasses firmly in place. She breathed a sigh of utter relief when she reached the elevator without encountering anybody asking questions about Anna Sinclair, a blessing considering her frame of mind.

The elevator opened and she stepped in. She turned around and a male hand—she could easily see it wasn't Ryan's—reached in and stopped the door from sliding closed. She shrank back into the corner, looked at the floor and shielded her face with the brim of her hat.

A person stepped into the elevator. Anna peeked up.

*Her father.*

Incredulous and angry and intensely disappointed at his appearance right on the heels of Ryan's bitter rejection, she literally couldn't speak.

"Anna," her father clipped. "What in the world have you done to your hair?"

She gave an unladylike but satisfying snort under her breath. "Well, hello to you, too, Dad. What are you doing here?" she asked, even though she had a pretty good idea.

He straightened his tie. "I think you know why I'm here. Your time's almost up."

Luckily she'd landed the Perfect Bridal account in the nick of time. She'd met the terms of their deal. She opened her mouth to tell him so, but the words wouldn't come.

The loss of Ryan's respect lay like a stone in her heart, making everything else in her world pale and insignificant. Suddenly her father's little deal seemed ridiculous, as did happily announcing that she'd landed an account so she would be able to meet his selfish terms and make a profit.

With crushing sadness filling her and the prospect of living the rest of her life without Ryan bearing down on her, meekly bowing down to her father's will bothered the hell out of her.

Suddenly everything was so clear, so very glaringly apparent. Losing Ryan had put everything in perspective, had shown her what was important and what wasn't.

Dear Lord, she'd *lost* what was important. She wasn't about to follow tradition and cave in to her father with that heartbreaking knowledge burning a hole in her heart.

It was time, finally, to stand up for what she wanted.

Why had it taken the death of her dream to be with Ryan to show her that?

Indignant fire roared through her. "You know, Dad," she said, stepping off the elevator when it stopped on her floor. "I've been thinking." She stopped next to her door, drew herself up and looked right at him. "Since when do you get to decide what I do with my life?"

He yanked his bushy gray eyebrows together and glared at her as he followed. "What the hell kind of question is that?"

She stuck her card key into the slot next to her hotel room door and yanked it out, finally determined to follow her own path. "It's one I should have asked

a year ago when we struck this stupid little deal.''
She stepped into her room, forcing her chin in the air.

"Stupid little deal," he blustered, trailing her in.
"Now, Anna, you agreed—"

"Yes, I did," she said, ruthlessly cutting him off.
"And I shouldn't have. I should be able to do what
I want with my life without having to fulfill some
ridiculous deal with you.''

He stared at her, shaking his head, then yanked his
conservative paisley tie loose. "What's come over
you, Anna?"

Oh, how to explain that when a heart is broken,
everything else seems pretty darn inconsequential?
But her father would never understand that; he knew
nothing about lost love. All he knew about was banking. Money. Status.

All of the things she didn't want to rely on to make
her way in the world.

"I guess maybe I've grown up, learned how to be
independent. Whatever the reason, I'm not going to
let you manipulate me any longer. I want to be a
wedding dress designer, not a banker." She looked
right into his eyes. "I need to follow my dream,
Dad."

He blinked and stared at her, then ran a hand
through his hair, making the perfectly combed gray
strands messy. "This is very important to you, isn't
it?"

She nodded. "I thought you knew that."

"I did, sort of. But…well, for you to stand up to
me like this…" He pulled his tie even looser. "I
guess I needed you to do that to prove how important
this bridal designer thing was."

Was that what this was all about? Growing a spine?

Thank heaven she'd somehow managed to do that. "You're a pretty hard man to stand up to, you know," she said, a hint of defensiveness in her voice.

He inclined his head, a ghost of a smile hovering on his lips. "I know. And I'm proud of you for finally doing it."

Bright, shining hope soared in her. "Proud enough to graciously let me go my own way? I'll do it either way, but I'd like to have your blessing."

"Anna, my girl," he said, his eyes glowing with what looked like…pride? "You've become quite independent and headstrong. I like that in a woman." He let out a heavy breath. "I guess I have no choice. If you want to be a wedding dress designer, be a wedding dress designer. I learned from your mother that dreams are important to follow. I'll have a heck of a time finding someone to fill your shoes at Sinclair Banking, but I'll have to try, won't I?"

Stunned, Anna fell back a step. "You're going to cut me loose from Sinclair Banking?"

He shrugged and held out both hands, palms up. "I guess I am. I'm proud of you, Anna."

His words melted a cold place inside of her and relief gushed through her. She'd stood up to him and he'd backed down. She was free to pursue her dream.

And while that was a welcome, long-awaited-for miracle, combining it with her heartbreak over losing Ryan's respect—and who knew what else—made her feel shaky and upset. "Thank you," she said, sinking down onto the bed. "I don't think I could have taken anything less from you right now."

He hunkered down, sincere caring glowing in his eyes for the first time in recent memory. "What's wrong?"

His apparent concern reminded her how much she needed a shoulder to lean on right now, no matter how unlikely and unexpected the shoulder might be. So she took a deep breath, said a silent prayer that her father's new attitude was genuine, and said, "I met a man."

He hesitated, then rose and lowered himself onto the bed next to her. "Why don't you tell me about it."

She looked around, wondering where to start. She cleared her throat, and then haltingly began to talk. Eventually she worked up her courage, and the story about Ryan came tumbling out, the whole thing, from how she'd met him to how he'd cut her from his life just two hours ago. When she finished talking, she let out a shaky breath.

Her father stood and paced around the room, then went over to the window and looked out, his hands shoved in his pants pockets. Dead silence reigned in the small hotel room.

He turned around and faced her. "So, do you love the guy?"

Trust him to cut right to the core of the matter and ask the difficult questions. In the face of his brutal query, she had to answer honestly. "I…do."

*But I shouldn't.* She rubbed a hand over her eyes, trying to erase Ryan from her brain, trying to make this as easy and as pain-free as possible on herself. The truth was, she'd blown it with Ryan, and how she felt might not matter in the least.

He snorted and shook his head. "Then what's the problem?"

She sighed raggedly. Trust her father to oversimplify the situation. Everything was black or white with him. She rose, fighting off the tears that had plagued her since Ryan had crushed her heart into tiny pieces and she'd walked out of his office. Cold reality settled down upon her.

Ryan didn't love her. Couldn't love her by his own admission. She lost the battle with her tears. Pressing her hand to her mouth, she turned away from her father, ashamed at her lack of control, something he'd always prized in himself.

Her father's voice jerked her back to reality. "You love this man. I'll ask again. What's the problem?"

She swiped the tears from her cheeks. "He doesn't love me, Dad."

"How do you know?"

She wheeled around. "He called me a rich, snooty princess. That doesn't sound like love to me."

Her father moved closer and touched her damp cheek. "People do strange things when they've been hurt. I think you should fight for him. I wish I had done that when I lost your mother."

Surprised, she looked up quick enough to see regret shining in his eyes. Realization dawned. "Why, you still love her, don't you?"

He nodded slowly, looking away, his mouth turned down into sad frown. "Yes, I do. But I was too stubborn and proud to fight for her when I needed to, and now it's too late. I've lost the only woman I'll ever love. I don't want you to have to live with the regret I do."

She looked at her dad again, and what she saw amazed and touched her. Standing before her was a human, vulnerable, fallible man who, even though he went about things in a wrong-headed way, hurt inside just like everybody else. His pain over losing her mother, and the fact that he'd shared it with her, cut into and remolded her perceptions of him.

She touched his arm. "Thank you for sharing that with me. I had no idea. I'll think about what you've said, all right?"

He nodded, then swiped a hand over his face, rubbing his eyes. He looked worn-out. "I'm registered at the hotel. I'm going to go to my room and make some calls, and then maybe later we can get together for dinner, all right? I've heard of a great restaurant in the Pearl District."

She walked him to the door, her mind overloaded, numb.

He awkwardly tugged her into his embrace. "I'm glad we worked this out."

"Me, too, Dad." She kissed his rough cheek, savoring their newfound closeness, hoping they'd reached a turning point in their relationship. She suspected she was going to need his shoulder in the future. "I...love you, Dad. We've had our problems in the past, but I want us to make a new start."

He kissed her cheek, his whiskers rubbing her jaw. "I want that, too."

He left and Anna walked over and wearily sank down onto the desk chair, almost unable to believe that the man who had just left the room was her father. Apparently her finally standing up to him had brought forth a stunning change within him and, hence, in their relationship.

Everything in her life had fallen into place.

Except Ryan. Dear, wonderful, exasperating Ryan.

She looked over and saw Nayr sitting on the bed. On shaking legs, she stood and moved over to pick him up. She pressed the soft little guy to her chest.

Her father's advice echoed through her brain.

*I think you should fight for this man.*

That he was still hurting over the loss of her mother's love deeply touched her and graphically illustrated the pain of lost, unfought-for-love.

A pain that she felt deeply right now, an ache she wasn't sure would ever go away unless she took her father's sage, spoken-from-experience advice.

Her father's regret-tinged voice rang in her head again.

*Don't make the same mistake I did.*

And then she heard Ryan telling her that she had thrown herself into a career designing wedding dresses, a symbol of one of the most romantic, love-filled events in any woman's life.

He'd pointed out something she'd wanted to ignore to stay emotionally safe: she was a romantic at heart. Her choice of a career proved that, just as he'd said.

And she *did* believe in love. She always had. She'd simply stifled her beliefs to keep her heart safe from the pain she'd always experienced in love.

Was she strong enough to let herself really feel love, embrace it?

And now, fight for it?

The icy-blue eyes Ryan had turned on her after he'd discovered her real identity appeared in her brain. She shivered. What if she failed and he looked at her that way again? A dull ache settled in her chest, snatching her breath away.

But not her nerve. What had Ryan said?

*Sometimes we have to face our fears.*

Yes. He'd taught her that. And the lonely, barren look in her father's eyes when he'd talked about losing her mother's love had shown her what could happen if she didn't fight for love, if she didn't face what scaréd her.

She'd stood up to her father and had taken her dream by the tail. Now it was time to go after another dream, one that had remained hidden inside of her, the victim of her fears.

It was well past time to go to battle for love.

# Chapter Eleven

After Ryan asked Anna to leave his office, he ignored the regret carving an abyss in his heart and ruthlessly immersed himself in work. He held a meeting with his department heads, made a few phone calls and scouted a location for a new store.

Long after the dinner hour, he returned home, exhausted, a dull hollowness he hated growing inside of him.

He halfheartedly ate a bowl of canned soup, more because he needed to eat rather than because he was really hungry. Brushing away the significance of not having a raging appetite, he sat at the counter, watery bowl of soup in front of him, and looked around his kitchen.

His empty, impersonal kitchen.

As if he had new eyes, he noticed the room didn't seem like a very homey place. With its bare counters, chrome-accented appliances and lack of décor it looked like he'd never even prepared a meal here, much less dropped even a single crumb on the floor. But now, after Anna had been here, lighting up the room with her presence, the kitchen looked sterile. Cold. Vacant.

He snorted under his breath. Damn. That's what he got for inviting a woman over.

Unable to stop his train of thought completely, he went back to Anna.

On cue, hot anger roared back to life inside of him. She'd lied to him, played him for a fool. But what really cut him to the core was the kind of woman she'd proven herself to be, one who manipulated others to get what she wanted.

His gut burned.

Thankfully he had a day full of meetings tomorrow to take his mind off her. He needed to regroup and work his tail off. That had always been his salvation; his job wouldn't fail him.

He dutifully ate his soup, then washed the bowl out and put it in the empty dishwasher, intending to lose himself in the work he'd brought home. The sales reports would keep him busy long into the night, ensuring that he'd sleep soundly, untormented by dreams of sweet-scented auburn hair, brown eyes and a smile that made his knees weak.

Before he could make his way to his laptop, the doorbell rang.

Frowning—who would be visiting this late?—he headed to the front door. Maybe his neighbor needed help with Max—    ·

His thoughts were cut off when he opened the door and saw Anna standing on the other side.

Surprise and pleasure ricocheted through him.

She looked…wonderful. She wore a short, light

blue clingy dress and a strappy pair of black sandals that highlighted her toned curves and got the blood moving around his body. She'd pulled her auburn hair up into a half bun that showed off her stunning bone structure and vivid brown eyes.

Unfortunately he had the absolutely stupid urge to pull her into his arms, hold her close and never let her go, despite the anger still smoldering inside of him.

After what she'd done, after he'd discovered the kind of manipulator she'd turned out to be, he shouldn't be so damned happy to see her.

He crammed his happiness into a ball and ignored it.

Anna wasn't a part of his life any more. He'd been dumb as hell letting himself get involved with her in the first place.

Regular working girl. Yeah, right.

She smiled tentatively. Nervously. "Hi."

He nodded, trying to ignore how awkward and apprehensive she looked. He failed. He *still* hated making her unhappy. Go figure. "Hello."

She shifted on her feet and bit her bottom lip. "Uh, can I come in?"

His first instinct was to say no and slam the door. He'd spent the whole day trying not to think about her; the last thing he needed was to have her here, messing with his senses, making him foolishly want her.

But the truth was, the uncomfortable, anxious look on her face nailed him right in the heart. What the hell. He let out a heavy breath, stepped back and made a sweeping gesture with his hand. "Come on in."

She stepped through the door, and her scent hit him like a solid wall of flowers—light, sexy. All Anna.

He swallowed and closed the door, feeling warm, wondering if there was something wrong with the air conditioning in his apartment.

*Get a grip.* All he had to do was remember that she was a rich princess who'd lied. Manipulated. Betrayed. Just like Sonya had. That bitter knowledge should be enough to keep his sanity.

Even when his sanity had always been in short supply around Anna.

He turned to her, wondering why she was here, wishing she wasn't. "What can I do for you?" he said, unable to erase a hint of ice from his voice. He never had been very good at hiding his emotions from her.

She brushed an errant strand of hair behind her ear. He could see her hands shaking. "I need to talk to you."

"Fire away," he said, hoping he didn't sound as curious as he was.

She cast her apprehensive gaze around. "C…could we sit down?"

"No. No way." He needed to keep this impersonal, and getting too cozy, seeing her in his personal space, would definitely blow that need to pieces. "I'd rather talk here."

She nodded, unsmiling. After a long silence, she said in a small voice, "You're mad at me, aren't you?"

"Hell, yes, I'm mad," he said without thinking, reacting to the red-hot anger she'd sent knifing through him when she'd revealed who she was.

Her eyes widened and shimmered and her lips quivered. She backed up a few steps.

Ah, damn. He was being a brute. "I mean—"

"No," she said, slicing the air with her hands. "Of course you're mad. I thought I could…" She trailed off, shaking her head, and pressed her fingers to the bridge of her nose. "I shouldn't have come here." She walked toward the door, her back straight, her movements rigid. "I'm sorry I bothered you."

"Wait." He touched her shoulder, feeling her warmth in every cell of his body, detecting her seductive scent in the air again.

She stiffened and remained silent, her head bent.

Even though he shouldn't care about any of this, even though he needed to cut her from his life quickly and efficiently, his curiosity exploded. "Why did you come here, Anna?"

*Because you love me?*

Crazy hope rocketed to life inside of him—

No. He wouldn't consider something that he could never allow to be. He shoved the irrelevant, ridiculous question out of his mind.

She made a noise in the back of her throat. "My father showed up, as I'd expected." She turned and looked at him, her lovely brown eyes piercing. "I landed the Perfect Bridal account, so technically I met the terms of his deal."

"I'm happy it all worked out for you." He drew in his brows. "But what does that have to do with your coming here?"

"I didn't tell him I'd met his terms. Instead I told him I was going to be a bridal designer, take it or leave it."

"Good for you," he said sincerely. Even though

he was angry with her for not sharing her true identity with him from the start, livid and wounded that she'd turned out to be a rich girl who couldn't be part of his life, he was glad her life was working out.

She was moving on. Without him. Maybe with some other guy…

Somehow, that thought dug deep, creating a flare of jealousy that surprised him.

"He told me about his lost love—my mother," she whispered, her words hanging in the air, so tempting…yet so frightening.

"And?" was all he said.

She sucked in a huge breath and looked right at him. "And I decided I didn't want to have a lost love of my own, that I had to face my fears and fight for what I wanted instead of backing down and running away from things that scare me." She gave him a watery half smile. "You taught me that, you know."

He didn't say anything. Couldn't say anything. Because while there was a part of him that was flattered and happy that she thought he was worth fighting for and that she'd learned something from him, another larger, smarter, learned-his-lesson-and-boy-was-he-not-going-to-go-there part knew he had to tell her that fighting for him was futile.

She'd sealed their fate the moment she'd deliberately hidden her true identity from him.

He looked at the floor, and then at her, a leaden sadness coming to life inside of him. She deserved his full attention now, his honesty. It wasn't what she wanted to hear, but it was all he could give; his heart was back where it belonged—off-limits. "Anna—"

"No, don't say it," she said, cutting him off. "I

can see this was a wasted trip. But I had to know. I've learned that I had to at least try.''

He nodded slowly. ''I wish things were different....''

''But they're not, are they?'' She put her small, soft hand on the bare skin of his arm for a moment, her eyes piercing, blatantly giving him one more chance.

Once again, her mesmerizing warmth seeped into him, reminding him how much he'd always wanted her. But in the end, when the chips were down, attraction and hormones didn't matter. The only thing that mattered was what lived inside of his battered, wary heart and made it impossible for him to set himself up to be hurt again.

Sonya and his parents had doled out enough cruel pain to last him a lifetime.

He forced himself to look right at her. ''No, things aren't different,'' he said in a low tone tinged with sadness. ''It kills me to hurt you, but I just can't ignore who you are and what you've done. I can't ignore my own need to protect myself.''

She nodded, pressing her lips together, her eyes filled with a deep sadness. ''That's what I thought.''

Silence hung over them for a few seconds, and then she abruptly turned and opened the door. ''Thank you for your honesty,'' she said in a wobbly voice, her back to him. ''I appreciate it.''

She stepped out into the hall, and a sudden, crazy panic filled him. He didn't want her to go, didn't want her to walk away and leave him, never to be seen again.

For a split second, he wanted to call her back. To hell with the past. But then an image of Sonya filled his brain and the idea died quickly. No, Anna had played him for a fool and shown him she had the power to hurt him. This was the way it had to be.

"Goodbye, Ryan." She turned and gave him a brave smile. "Have a good life."

He watched her walk down the hall to the elevator, his chest filled with a sudden, fiery ache.

And then she stepped into the elevator and walked out of his life forever.

The words *I'm sorry* echoed in his head.

But he wasn't saying them to Anna.

He was saying them to himself.


"I hit it! I hit it!" Juan cried, jumping up and down, pointing across the park in the direction he'd hit the baseball. "Did you see that, Wyan?"

Ryan smiled and gave Juan a thumbs up, hoping the speech therapy classes he'd enrolled him in would show results soon. "I sure did. That'd be a homer for sure."

"I want to do it again, lots of times." Juan assumed the odd batting stance he'd adopted, his jeans-clad rear stuck way out. "Can I hit again, Wyan? Please?"

"You can hit it as many times as you want, after we eat," Ryan said, heading toward the blanket he'd spread out in the grass. He gestured to the ball. "Go get the ball, okay, buddy? I'm starved," he lied. His normally healthy appetite had ceased to exist.

Juan frowned and hung his head, but started in the direction of the ball. "Okay. But I'm eating fast so I can hit lots more."

Ryan shook his head, grinning, proud of the way Juan had taken to baseball. The kid was a natural and should be on a Little League team, an experience

Ryan had missed out on because his parents couldn't afford the fee or take the time to sign him up and go to games. He made a mental note to look into that for Juan. Every child should be able to play baseball in the warm spring air, or in the case of Oregon, the cold spring rain.

With the warm June sun beating down on his back, Ryan opened the cooler and set out the deli sandwiches, drinks and potato chips he'd bought premade at the store, his mood lightening a bit. Maybe being with the little guy, teaching him how to hit and catch, would help get rid of the pall that had come down on Ryan since Anna had left his apartment yesterday, her eyes glazed with unhappiness.

Damn, he hoped so. He wanted to obliterate the ache in his soul with everything in him, the pain that had burned inside of him since she'd confessed her real identity.

Anna Sinclair. Major heiress. He should be thinking about *that*—who she really was, the kind of woman she'd turned out to be. Instead, since she'd come to fight for him, opening floodgates he couldn't seem to stop, he found himself remembering her sweet smile, delicate scent and strong-willed determination to succeed, which, surprisingly, had become even more impressive since he'd found out who she was. As Anna Sinclair, she could sit around and eat bonbons all day.

Instead she'd bravely embarked on a quest for a career as a bridal designer as working girl Anna Simpson, determined to succeed without her family name backing her up. Even more impressive, when she could have easily fallen back on clinching the Perfect Bridal account, she hadn't. No. She'd stood up to her father and demanded her right to follow her dream. As much as Ryan didn't want to, he admired the hell out of her for that.

But admiring her didn't change anything. He might eventually be able to forgive her for lying to him, but he would never be able to forget that she was exactly the kind of woman he'd sworn never to get tangled up with again. He could never allow himself to love her.

Juan came bounding up, the baseball in his hands. "Here it is, Wyan." He dropped the ball on the ground and plopped down on the blanket next to Ryan. "When can we play some more?"

Ryan put a small ham sandwich and some chips on a plate and handed it to Juan. "You gotta eat if you're going to be a big-time baseball player." He noticed Juan's grubby hands, wishing he'd had the brains to bring some antibacterial cleanser.

"Hey, bud, let's wipe your hands."

Juan held out his hands, and Ryan dampened a paper napkin on the ice in the cooler and wiped them off as best he could. "There you go. Dig in."

Juan picked up the sandwich and took a bite. "Yeah, I know I gotta eat," he mumbled around the food. "But it's just so neat, hitting the ball and watching it fly."

Ryan shoved a straw in a juice-box, Juan's favorite drink, and set it on the blanket. "Thirsty? There's a juice box."

Juan grabbed the box and downed the whole thing in one long swig, then attacked the chips, chattering on and on about baseball, a girl in his class who could bend her arm the wrong way—cool, huh?—and a grasshopper he'd found but had to let go.

Ryan opened another juice-box for Juan and half-heartedly ate his sandwich, letting Juan talk, enjoying the kid's view of the world and silly stories.

At one point, Juan hesitated and looked up at him, his big, brown eyes sad, and said, "My gwanny is sick, isn't she?"

Ryan's stomach tightened. "Yes, she is, buddy. Her arthritis is flaring up, and she has an infection in her tummy that's making her sick." Juan's granny had been admitted into the hospital yesterday and Juan had been temporarily moved into emergency foster care. Luckily the arrangement had worked out well. Juan had been to this foster house before and was familiar with and liked the people who lived there.

Ryan cleared his throat. "Juan, I saw your grand-mother in the hospital this morning, and she gave me permission to tell you something very important."

Juan stopped chewing and looked up at him. "Is it bad?" he asked in a small voice, his face serious, his eyes large.

"No, no, bud," Ryan said, his heart twisting. Juan had had to deal with too many bad things in his young life, just like Ryan had. He took Juan's small hand in his and squeezed. "I think it's very good. You know your friend Kenny from school?"

Juan nodded.

"Well, Kenny's parents have decided that they want to adopt you."

Juan broke out into a huge smile. "Weally? They're neat. I went there once for a birfday party, and they have a big house, and a yard and a big, black dog who catches the Fwisbee when I throw it."

"Well, pretty soon, that will be your house and

your dog, Juan,'' he told him, glad that he'd checked out the family for himself and was satisfied they would give Juan the love and stability he deserved. ''They're very anxious to have you come and join the family.''

Juan stood, his face wreathed in smiles, and jumped up and down and flailed his arms around. ''Yippee!'' he crowed, running in circles. ''I'm going to have a weal family, and Kenny will be my weal bother, and I'll have a weal dog, and a weal yard. Yippee, Yip—'' He stopped and stared at Ryan, concern growing in his brown eyes. ''But what about you, Wyan?''

Ryan jerked his eyebrows together. ''What do you mean? I'll still come visit you.''

Juan slowly knelt and touched Ryan's hand, suddenly looking very miserable and very, very serious for a six-year-old. ''When I get 'dopted I'll have a family, and you'll be all alone.''

Ryan's chest tightened as if he had a vise clamped around him.

*All alone.*

The words echoed through his hollow heart, creating an icy void he wasn't sure he could ever fill.

He forced his mouth into a smile and rubbed Juan's thin shoulder. ''Aw, bud, don't worry about me.'' The last thing he wanted to do was ruin Juan's happy day with his own problems. ''I'll be fine, and I'll still come see you all the time. All right? And as soon as your granny is well, I'm sure she'll come see you, too.'' Thank heaven Juan's drug-head, convict parents had permanently signed away their parental rights.

Juan stood up and stared at Ryan, his deep brown eyes reflecting something Ryan had never seen there before. Before he could figure out what the look meant, Juan plastered himself against Ryan's chest, squeezing his thin arms around Ryan's neck. "I love you, Wyan."

Ryan froze briefly, feeling Juan's trusting, warm, angular body next to his. He slowly put his arms around Juan and squeezed him tight, trying to absorb all the good things this one little boy had brought into his life. "I love you, too, buddy," he whispered, his voice husky, meaning it with everything in him. Warmth filled his chest.

Juan pulled away and patted Ryan's cheek. "If you get lonely, maybe you can come and live with Kenny and me." And then he ran off, flinging the baseball in the air.

"Stay where I can see you!" Ryan managed to call to Juan.

He then sat on the blanket, one elbow propped on a raised knee, his mind spinning, his heart full and complete and warm.

He rubbed his forehead. He'd been so damn sure that the lack of love in his life proved love wasn't real and that he would never, ever feel it. Sure, he'd offhandedly told Anna he loved Juan, but he hadn't been sure he really did. He hadn't, he realized, known what love felt like.

Now he knew, unequivocally, that he loved Juan. There was no mistaking the warm, wonderful feeling filling his heart to overflowing, warming him from the inside out.

Love did exist.

Juan's genuine love and honesty had opened up Ryan's heart and shown him the truth. He genuinely loved Juan, cared about him, wanted what was best for him.

Ryan smiled, liking the feeling of actually loving someone and embracing the emotion wholeheartedly. But his mood fell when he realized that Juan was right about one thing. Even though Ryan would continue to see Juan whenever he could, Ryan would be, for the most part, all alone. Sure, he had his business to keep him busy, and he loved to ride his motorcycle, and had a few buddies who he hung out with occasionally. And he certainly had plenty of money to travel the world. But now, the thought of being truly solitary for the rest of his life created a huge blank space inside of him.

*Anna.*

Her name popped into his head, and as much as he hated to admit it, he'd been happier than he could ever remember being with her. He'd looked forward to her laughter, her kisses, her mere presence.

Just the thought of never seeing her again left a familiar sick feeling in the pit of his belly. Even though her deception and revelation of her real identity had burned him to the core, she had filled up his life with warmth and companionship and a simple happiness and contentment he'd never felt before.

Would he ever feel those things again?

Dread, pure, real and pretty damn frightening, moved through him, setting his nerves on a hard edge. He deliberately brought to mind the profound lesson Juan had taught him.

Love existed.

If he knew where to look.

If he knew how to forget his past and embrace it.

All at once, it was as if all lingering bits of pain and betrayal from his past magically disintegrated, finally freeing his heart, allowing him to see what was important—and what wasn't.

Love wasn't something he could or couldn't *allow*. It lived inside of him, a living, breathing thing, existing on its own whether he acknowledged it or not.

Love just was.

Thankful he'd discovered the truth, he glanced at his watch, filled with a do-or-die anticipation. He had to return Juan to his temporary foster home in an hour. After that, Ryan had something important to do, something that couldn't wait.

Something that had the power to change his life—good or bad—forever.

Because Juan had taught him that the love inside of him wasn't so unfamiliar after all.

And he knew exactly where he needed to look now.

He only hoped he hadn't made the discovery too damn late.

What if Anna had changed her mind?

Ryan dropped off Juan at his foster home with the brand new baseball mitt, ball, and glove Ryan had bought for him, along with a promise to play more baseball—all day long—tomorrow.

Ryan then quickly headed home and traded his car in favor of his motorcycle. He needed to feel the summer wind on his face, needed the sense of freedom and calm riding his bike always brought him to counteract the ominous dread creeping into him by the second. Within minutes, he was headed to Anna's hotel, but the calm his bike usually caused was obliterated by the anxious thoughts ping-ponging around inside his brain.

What if she was gone?

He'd go after her.

What if she didn't want him after his callous, weak-willed, wrongheaded behavior last night?

He'd do everything in his power to change her mind.

What if that didn't work?

He refused to consider that. He'd finally discovered that the only thing that mattered was that he loved Anna.

No matter who she was.

He wasn't about to give up now.

Filled with an impending sense of doom, he parked his bike in a No Parking zone at the front of the hotel and hurried into the lobby, praying Anna hadn't checked out. He went directly to the front desk to ask if she was still registered. But before he could ask the question, a man stepped up next to him.

"Aren't you Ryan Cavanaugh?" the man asked. "I recognize you from the pictures in the paper."

Ryan looked at the impeccably dressed, gray-haired man. Familiar brown eyes stared back at him. A vague sense of recognition shot through him. He lowered his brows. "Do I know you?"

The other man extended his hand. "Peter Sinclair."

Ryan's mouth went dry. "Of course." He shook the proffered hand. "Your daughter has your eyes."

"My one contribution. Her mother gets the rest of the credit."

Ryan looked around. "Listen, I don't mean to be rude, but—"

"You're looking for her, aren't you?"

Ryan nodded and unbuttoned his leather jacket, feeling warm. This was Anna's father, the one person besides her who might be able to make or break his chances with her. "Yes, I am."

Mr. Sinclair leaned one elbow on the front desk and skewered him with his dark eyes. "Do you love her?" he asked bluntly.

"I do, sir," Ryan said without hesitation. He had Juan to thank for pounding some sense into him. How did the saying go? Out of the mouths of babes?

Mr. Sinclair nodded to the bellman's station. "That's her luggage there."

Ryan looked at the navy blue matched set and swallowed heavily. His heart squeezed. "She's leaving?"

Mr. Sinclair rolled his eyes. "I'm not sure what she's doing. We were getting ready to go to the airport, but the strangest thing happened. She took a teddy bear from her luggage—called the thing *Nayr* for heaven sake—and said she needed to go to some Rose Park." He gazed speculatively at Ryan. "Does that mean anything to you?"

The bear he'd won for her at the Festival Center.

Raw hope trickled through Ryan. He stared at Mr. Sinclair. "What did you say she called the bear?"

"Nayr. Strangest thing I've ever heard. She said the name had some personal significance..." He trailed off, then tilted his head and shrugged. "Of course, she's been picking odd names for her stuffed animals since she was a little girl. Had a stuffed hippo she called Retep. I always wondered how she came up with that name."

Ryan tuned out Sinclair, going over the bear's name in his head. Nair? Like the hair remover? No. Maybe Nayr...

*N A Y R.* He spelled it over and over again in his

head, remembering what Anna had told him about how she'd named her stuffed animals after people she cared about when she was a child.

*Ryan.* Spelled backward! Yes!

It was a dumb thing to hold on to, but it was all he had. Anna had named the bear after him. And she hadn't left town yet. He looked at her father. "Yes, sir it does mean something to me. Maybe everything." He backed away, holding up a hand. "Thanks. You'll never know how much this means to me."

Mr. Sinclair inclined his head. "Oh, I know, trust me." He gave Ryan a tight smile. "Just don't hurt my little girl again, all right?"

Ryan smiled grimly back, hoping he had the chance to make up for how much he'd already hurt her. "Oh, you can be sure I won't." And he meant it. When he thought about how he'd turned her away last night he wanted to kick himself until he was black and blue.

He turned and sprinted out the hotel door. Within seconds he was on his bike, heading toward the Rose Garden Park.

But before he'd ridden a block, he took a quick detour to a little store he'd seen on the way to the hotel. After a few minutes of frenzied searching in the store for the right item, he paid the cashier and hopped back on his bike, a small parcel tucked into the front of his leather jacket. As he sped to the park, breaking every speed limit along the way, he prayed with everything in him that her naming the bear after him was a positive sign.

And that Anna hadn't gone to the place they'd met to say goodbye.

To him.

* * *

"Well, Nayr, I'm not exactly sure what I'm doing here," Anna said to the Teddy bear she held in her lap. "I should be leaving." She sat on the stairs leading down to the Rose Garden, adjacent to the exact spot where she and Ryan had first met and where she'd fallen over in her wedding gown.

The place where she'd first seen Ryan, looking like her dream come true with his gold hair gleaming in the sun, his masculine body so wonderfully displayed by his black tux.

He'd taken her breath away that day.

And taken so much more since.

Even so, she'd been prepared to leave Portland and Ryan behind and put an end to this heart-wrenching chapter in her life. Despite the ache inside of her telling her she was doing the wrong thing by leaving without fighting harder for Ryan, without demanding he give them a chance.

She'd been in a crazy, incredibly irritating kind of push-pull limbo since last night. A place where she wanted desperately to follow her heart but was simply too afraid to take the risk once again since Ryan had rejected her. Too afraid of putting herself in a place where she might hurt more than she already did, although she wondered if that was possible.

But when she'd reached the lobby to go to the airport, reality had set in, and a kind of panic had taken over her. Something deep inside of her had trembled and balked, and she'd desperately needed to come here, the place where it had all started between her and Ryan. She had to make a decision.

A decision that could change her life.

She looked down at the fluffy little bear, his fur

turned to almost the same gold as Ryan's hair in the sun.

*Sometimes you have to face your fears.*

Ryan's words echoed in her head again, on instant replay. She smiled, her eyes burning, remembering how afraid she'd been on the Ferris wheel at the Festival Center and how Ryan had said those exact words and coaxed her to open her eyes and take in the wonderful view. When she had finally mustered up the courage to look, it was as if they'd been floating above the rest of the world, high up in a place she'd never been brave enough to experience before.

Despite her fear, she'd loved the experience. She had been so glad she'd taken Ryan's advice and opened her eyes.

Was it time to open her eyes now and enjoy the "view"? Was it time to finally take her romantic idealism to heart, the bone-deep principles she'd stifled, and really fight for the man she loved instead of scurrying away when things got tough? If she didn't, she'd have nothing. If she did...well, she might end up with Ryan.

Her heart raced.

With Ryan!

She'd been wearing a veil in this very spot the day she'd met him and she saw now that she'd been wearing it—hiding behind it, actually—ever since. It had made her world safe...but hazy and out-of-focus and distorted. She hadn't seen anything in its true light since.

Until now. That cursed veil had been ripped from over her eyes and she could finally see the world as it was.

A world where the only important thing was that she loved Ryan.

It was up to her to convince him, no matter what, that he had to give them a chance.

She'd thought she was so brave last night, facing her fear and going to Ryan's apartment. But she hadn't been brave for very long. She'd run as fast as she could when he hadn't fallen at her feet, confessing his undying love. She simply gave up.

Now was the time to really put her brand new spine to the test.

Filled with a wonderful, calming sense of purpose that had been absent from her life for far too long, she stood, smoothing her yellow linen pants, noticing how warm the sun was on her shoulders, how blue the sky above her was. Feeling reborn, she clutched Nayr to her chest and moved past vibrantly colored, heavily fragrant rosebushes and up another set of stone stairs that led to the half-empty parking lot.

As she turned toward her car, a low, growling hum caught her ear. She paused at the top of the stairs, her heart suddenly pounding.

A motorcycle.

Ryan?

No, she was imagining things, imagining that he was going to show up like a knight in shiny leather and tell her he loved her more than anything, that he couldn't live without her.

It was her job to take control and convince him of that.

The motorcycle came into view. She squinted, ridiculously trying to discern if the rider was indeed Ryan. But she'd never actually seen his motorcycle and the person—yes, yes, it was a man!—was indistinguishable in the black helmet and leather jacket he wore.

It could be any guy out for a ride through the park on a sunny summer day.

She waited, though, her newly freed love and self-understanding blossoming at last inside of her like one of the beautiful roses surrounding her. She was rooted to the spot, hoping, praying....

The man on the motorcycle slowed as he rolled near, then put his feet down, his muscled legs bulging underneath his grass-stained jeans. He slowly turned off the bike.

She stared. All she could hear was the frantic beating of her heart.

In slow motion, the man reached up and unhooked his helmet. And then he took it off, slowly exposing a chiseled, tanned jaw, incredibly gorgeous deep blue eyes, and golden hair the color of the Teddy bear clutched in her arms.

Her heart melted.

He swung one leg over the bike, cocked the kickstand, and said, "Hey, pretty lady, want a ride?" He smiled, showing straight, white teeth and that darn dimple. He patted the bike's seat. "There's plenty of room."

She slowly walked over to him, feeling like she was floating instead of actually touching the ground. "Oh, I don't know, mister. I'm not supposed to talk to strangers."

He pulled something from the front of his leather jacket. "Well," he drawled, holding up a small Teddy bear, its fur almost the exact shade of her dyed hair, a white lace bow around its chubby neck. "I think my bear, Anna, knows your bear, Nayr. Is that good enough?''

Instantly, hot, insistent tears pressed on the backs of her eyelids.

He'd named the bear Anna.

Shaking, Anna looked at him and then the bear he held. She had to be sure Ryan knew who the woman standing before him really was and that he wanted Anna Sinclair as much as he wanted Anna Simpson.

Before she could speak, he said, ''This bear is Anna. It's the same backward as it is forward. So I guess the two of them are the same, aren't they?'' he asked, moving closer, his voice like rough silk. ''Either name will do.''

He understood.

Trembling, wanting to believe what she thought he was saying but so unsure of *everything* despite her newfound bravery, so ashamed that she'd deceived him, she stood frozen, unable to move. Tears crested in her eyes and ran down her cheeks. ''I'm so sorry I lied—''

''Shh,'' he said, reaching out for her. His big, strong hands wrapped around her shoulders and pulled her to him. He pressed his mouth to hers and kissed her lips gently, almost reverently. ''I was a fool to let you go, Anna.''

She clung to him, breathing in his scent. ''I can't believe you came for me.''

He pressed a finger on her lips, his eyes full of regret. ''Stop. Don't say anything else. I was a damn idiot for letting what happened in my past keep me from admitting my true feelings, for letting you walk away.'' He closed his eyes briefly. ''I couldn't see that I fell in love with what's inside of you and that whether you were an heiress or not didn't matter. I couldn't see the truth and say the words."

She bit her lip, wanting to believe him with everything in her. "And are you ready to do that now?" She searched his face for trace of doubt. She found none.

He bent close and gently kissed her mouth again, then buried his face in her hair. "I love you, Anna Sinclair, no matter who you are, more than anything in the world. Nothing matters but that you complete me and make me the happiest man on earth."

Her chest bursting with long awaited happiness, she looked at Ryan. Miraculously she finally saw pure, unmistakable love shining in his eyes like a bright beacon glowing in the night, meant only for her. "Oh, Ryan, I love you, too! I've made some mistakes, also, and I see now that I was using my past as a shield to shut you out." She smiled and caressed his rough jaw. "It was easy to hold on to the fantasy of love by designing wedding dresses, but admitting to feeling it is what counts."

He stared deep into her eyes and ran his hand across her lips, caressing gently, reverently. "From now on, you're the most important thing in my life."

She nodded and tugged his head down for another kiss. "I'd better be, mister," she said, smiling against his mouth. "I'll be sure and remind you if you ever forget that."

"I'll never forget." He smoothed her hair away from her face and looked deep into her eyes. "Trust me. I may be a slow study, but I never forget what I've learned. How about we have a real wedding," he murmured, kissing her face. "Will you marry me?"

Unadulterated bliss stole through her. Ryan's wife. Her very own real wedding. Her dream come true. "Yes," she whispered, smiling up at him. "Yes, of course I'll marry you." She couldn't believe that she and Ryan had found a way to love each other and would be planning their very own Bridal Chronicle. A real one this time. As real as the love she'd waited so long to discover.

And then he pulled her close and bent his head and whispered in her ear over and over again how much he loved and adored her.

And she finally knew where she belonged. In his arms. Her heart next to his.

Forever.

\* \* \* \* \*

*If you enjoyed THE BRIDAL CHRONICLES, you will love Lissa Manley's next book for Silhouette Romance:*

*THE BABY CHRONICLES*

*Coming in January 2004!*

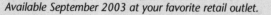

If you enjoyed what you just read,
then we've got an offer you can't resist!

# Take 2 bestselling love stories FREE!

# Plus get a FREE surprise gift!

Clip this page and mail it to Silhouette Reader Service™

| IN U.S.A. | IN CANADA |
|---|---|
| 3010 Walden Ave. | P.O. Box 609 |
| P.O. Box 1867 | Fort Erie, Ontario |
| Buffalo, N.Y. 14240-1867 | L2A 5X3 |

**YES!** Please send me 2 free Silhouette Romance® novels and my free surprise gift. After receiving them, if I don't wish to receive anymore, I can return the shipping statement marked cancel. If I don't cancel, I will receive 6 brand-new novels every month, before they're available in stores! In the U.S.A., bill me at the bargain price of $3.34 plus 25¢ shipping and handling per book and applicable sales tax, if any*. In Canada, bill me at the bargain price of $3.80 plus 25¢ shipping and handling per book and applicable taxes**. That's the complete price and a savings of at least 10% off the cover prices—what a great deal! I understand that accepting the 2 free books and gift places me under no obligation ever to buy any books. I can always return a shipment and cancel at any time. Even if I never buy another book from Silhouette, the 2 free books and gift are mine to keep forever.

215 SDN DNUM
315 SDN DNUN

| Name | (PLEASE PRINT) | |
|---|---|---|
| Address | Apt.# | |
| City | State/Prov. | Zip/Postal Code |

\* Terms and prices subject to change without notice. Sales tax applicable in N.Y.
\*\* Canadian residents will be charged applicable provincial taxes and GST.
    All orders subject to approval. Offer limited to one per household and not valid to current Silhouette Romance® subscribers.
    ® are registered trademarks of Harlequin Books S.A., used under license.

SROM02                              ©1998 Harlequin Enterprises Limited

✂

**Your opinion is important to us!** Please take a few moments to share your thoughts with us about your experiences with Harlequin and Silhouette books. Your comments will be very useful in ensuring that we deliver books you love to read. *Please take a few minutes to complete the questionnaire, then send it to us at the address below.*

---

Send your completed questionnaires to:
**Harlequin/Silhouette Reader Survey, P.O. Box 9046, Buffalo, NY 14269-9046**

---

1. As you may know, there are many different lines under the Harlequin and Silhouette brands. Each of the lines is listed below. Please check the box that most represents your reading habit for each line.

| Line | Currently read this line | Do not read this line | Not sure if I read this line |
|------|--------------------------|-----------------------|------------------------------|
| Harlequin American Romance | ❏ | ❏ | ❏ |
| Harlequin Duets | ❏ | ❏ | ❏ |
| Harlequin Romance | ❏ | ❏ | ❏ |
| Harlequin Historicals | ❏ | ❏ | ❏ |
| Harlequin Superromance | ❏ | ❏ | ❏ |
| Harlequin Intrigue | ❏ | ❏ | ❏ |
| Harlequin Presents | ❏ | ❏ | ❏ |
| Harlequin Temptation | ❏ | ❏ | ❏ |
| Harlequin Blaze | ❏ | ❏ | ❏ |
| Silhouette Special Edition | ❏ | ❏ | ❏ |
| Silhouette Romance | ❏ | ❏ | ❏ |
| Silhouette Intimate Moments | ❏ | ❏ | ❏ |
| Silhouette Desire | ❏ | ❏ | ❏ |

2. Which of the following best describes why you bought *this book?* One answer only, please.

| | | | |
|---|---|---|---|
| the picture on the cover | ❏ | the title | ❏ |
| the author | ❏ | the line is one I read often | ❏ |
| part of a miniseries | ❏ | saw an ad in another book | ❏ |
| saw an ad in a magazine/newsletter | ❏ | a friend told me about it | ❏ |
| I borrowed/was given this book | ❏ | other: _____ | ❏ |

3. Where did you buy *this book?* One answer only, please.

| | | | |
|---|---|---|---|
| at Barnes & Noble | ❏ | at a grocery store | ❏ |
| at Waldenbooks | ❏ | at a drugstore | ❏ |
| at Borders | ❏ | on eHarlequin.com Web site | ❏ |
| at another bookstore | ❏ | from another Web site | ❏ |
| at Wal-Mart | ❏ | Harlequin/Silhouette Reader | ❏ |
| at Target | ❏ | Service/through the mail | |
| at Kmart | ❏ | used books from anywhere | ❏ |
| at another department store or mass merchandiser | ❏ | I borrowed/was given this book | ❏ |

4. On average, how many Harlequin and Silhouette books do you buy at one time?

I buy _____ books at one time ❏
I rarely buy a book ❏

MRQ403SR-1A

5. How many times per month do you shop for any *Harlequin and/or Silhouette* books? One answer only, please.

    1 or more times a week   ❑     a few times per year   ❑

    1 to 3 times per month   ❑     less often than once a year   ❑

    1 to 2 times every 3 months   ❑     never   ❑

6. When you think of your ideal heroine, which *one* statement describes her the best? One answer only, please.

    She's a woman who is strong-willed   ❑     She's a desirable woman   ❑

    She's a woman who is needed by others   ❑     She's a powerful woman   ❑

    She's a woman who is taken care of   ❑     She's a passionate woman   ❑

    She's an adventurous woman   ❑     She's a sensitive woman   ❑

7. The following statements describe types or genres of books that you may be interested in reading. Pick *up to 2 types* of books that you are most interested in.

    I like to read about truly romantic relationships   ❑

    I like to read stories that are sexy romances   ❑

    I like to read romantic comedies   ❑

    I like to read a romantic mystery/suspense   ❑

    I like to read about romantic adventures   ❑

    I like to read romance stories that involve family   ❑

    I like to read about a romance in times or places that I have never seen   ❑

    Other: _____   ❑

*The following questions help us to group your answers with those readers who are similar to you. Your answers will remain confidential.*

8. Please record your year of birth below.

    19 _____

9. What is your marital status?

    single  ❑     married  ❑     common-law  ❑     widowed  ❑

    divorced/separated  ❑

10. Do you have children 18 years of age or younger currently living at home?

    yes  ❑     no  ❑

11. Which of the following best describes your employment status?

    employed full-time or part-time  ❑     homemaker  ❑     student  ❑

    retired  ❑     unemployed  ❑

12. Do you have access to the Internet from either home or work?

    yes  ❑     no  ❑

13. Have you ever visited eHarlequin.com?

    yes  ❑     no  ❑

14. What state do you live in?

    _____

15. Are you a member of Harlequin/Silhouette Reader Service?

    yes  ❑     Account # _____     no  ❑     MRQ403SR-1B

SILHOUETTE *Romance*®

# COMING NEXT MONTH

### #1690 HER PREGNANT AGENDA—Linda Goodnight
*Marrying the Boss's Daughter*

General Counsel Grant Lawson agreed to protect
Ariana Fitzpatrick—and her unborn twins—from her custody-
seeking, two-timing ex-fiancé. But delivering the precious
babies and kissing their oh-so-beautiful mother senseless
weren't in his job description! And falling in love—well,
that *definitely* wasn't part of the agenda!

### #1691 THE VISCOUNT & THE VIRGIN—Valerie Parv
*The Carramer Trust*

Legend claimed anyone who served the Merrisand Trust would
find true love, but the only thing Rowe Sevrin, Viscount Aragon,
found was feisty, fiery-haired temptress Kirsten Bond. How
could his reluctant assistant seem so innocent and inexperienced
and still be a mother? And why was her young son Rowe's spit-
ting image?

### #1692 THE MOST ELIGIBLE DOCTOR
—Karen Rose Smith

Nurse Brianne Barrington had lost every person she'd ever
loved. So when she took the job with Jed Sawyer, a rugged,
capable doctor with emotional wounds of his own, she intended
to keep her distance. But Jed's tender embraces awakened a
womanly desire she'd never felt before. Could the cautious,
love-wary Brianna risk her heart again?

### #1693 MARLIE'S MYSTERY MAN—Doris Rangel
*Soulmates*

Marlie Simms was falling for two men—sort of! One man
was romantic, sexy and funny, and the other was passionate,
determined and strong. Except they were *both* Caid Matthews—
a man whose car accident left his spirit split in two! And only
Marlie's love could make Caid a whole man again....

SRCNM0903

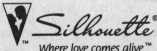